FEMME

A "Nameless Detective" Novella

Bill Pronzini

FEMME

A "Nameless Detective" Novella

Bill Pronzini

CEMETERY DANCE PUBLICATIONS

Baltimore
❖ 2012 ❖

FIRST EDITION
ISBN: 978-1-58767-267-5
Cemetery Dance Publications Edition 2012

Femme
Copyright © 2012 Bill Pronzini
Dust jacket illustration by Glen Orbik
Dust jacket design by Gail Cross
Typesetting and book design by Robert Morrish
All rights reserved. Manufactured in the United States of America

Cemetery Dance Publications
132-B Industry Lane, Unit 7
Forest Hill, MD 21050
Email: info@cemeterydance.com
www.cemeterydance.com

Dedication

For Rich Chizmar, with thanks
for inviting *Nameless* and me
to do a little Cemetery Dance

1.

Femme fatale. French for "deadly woman."

You hear the term a lot these days, usually in connection with noir fiction and film noir. Brigid O'Shaughnessy in *The Maltese Falcon*. Cora in *The Postman Always Rings Twice*. Phyllis Dietrichson in *Double Indemnity*. Matty Walker in *Body Heat*. Catherine Tramell in *Basic Instinct*. Scheming, sexually demanding women who ensnare their lovers in bonds of irresistible and destructive desire. Lethal women. Eve in the Garden, Jezebel, Salome, Cleopatra.

But they're not just products of literature, film, the folklore of nearly every culture. They exist in modern society, too. The genuine femmes fatale you hear about now and then are every bit as evil as the fictional variety. Yet what sets them apart is that they're the failures, the ones who for one reason or another got caught. For every one of those, there must be several times as many who get away with their destructive crimes.

In the dozen years I spent in law enforcement and the thirty years I've been a private investigator, I never once had the misfortune to cross paths with this type of seductress. Never expected to. Never thought much about the breed except when confronted with one in a film or the pages of a book or the pulp magazines I collect. Female monsters of a different variety, yes, like the pair I'd encountered not long ago who made a living murdering elderly people for their money. But a real femme fatale in the classic mode? Not even close. If you'd told me one day I would, and that her brand of evil would be like nothing I could ever have imagined, I'd have laughed and said no way.

I'm not laughing now.

Neither is Jake Runyon. He was in it, too, not quite from the beginning but all the way to the end. He'd never come across anyone like her, either, and it left him as shaken as it did me.

Her name was Cory Beckett. Real name, not an alias. A deadly woman who brought a couple of new twists to the species.

New—and terrible.

2.

I met Cory Beckett in a routine fashion, and came away from that first meeting with no real inkling of her true nature.

She was not the sort of woman who usually sought my services. In her late twenties—twenty-eight, I found out later. Strikingly attractive, her sex appeal the low-key, smoldering variety. Sitting demurely in Abe Melikian's private office, the first time I laid eyes on her, dressed in an expensive caramel-colored suit and a high-necked, green silk blouse. The outfit, and the fili-greed gold and ruby ring on her little finger, indicated she was well fixed financially; always a plus in a prospective client.

She had thick, wavy black hair, a mod-el's willowy figure, and a worried smile that even tuned down had a good deal of candle-power. But what you noticed first, and re-membered most vividly, were her luminous gray-green eyes. They had a powerful magnetic quality; I could feel the pull of them, like being drawn into dark, calm water. It was only when you got to know her that you realized the calm surface was a lie—that underneath there weren't just smoldering sexual fires but riptides and whirlpools and hungry darting things with teeth.

It was Melikian who'd called me to set up the meeting. He was one of the more successful bail bondsmen in the city, with half a dozen employees and offices across Bryant Street from the Hall of Justice. I'd done a fair amount of work for him over the years, to our mutual satisfaction and trust. All he'd said on the phone, in his typically gruff way, was that the matter involved a possible bail forfeiture.

Melikian hated jumpers, as he called them, even more than other bondsmen. To hear him tell it, they were all part of a vast conspiracy to ruin his business and drive him into bankruptcy. As a result he was careful to avoid posting bond for anyone who struck him as a potential flight risk, but now and then he got burned anyway. Usually when that happened, he ranted and raved and threatened dire consequences. Not this time. When I sat down with him and Cory Beckett, he was meek as a mouse.

She was the reason. Those eyes and that sleek body of hers had worked their spell on him; he hung on her every word, and the gleam in his eye when he looked at her was anything but cynical. An even more telling measure of how she'd affected him was an unprecedented willingness to split my fee with her.

She let him do most of the talking at first. The subject was her brother, Kenneth Beckett, who'd been arrested and arraigned six weeks ago on a grand theft charge. The bail amount was a cool $100,000, which meant she'd had to put up the usual ten percent commission in cash plus some kind of collateral for most or all of the rest. I didn't ask what the collateral was, figuring that it was none of my concern.

"The trial's ten days off yet," Melikian said, "so we got that long to save the bond and kid's tail. But technically he's already a jumper on account of one of the terms the judge set for his bail."

"Which is?"

"Not allowed to leave the city without police permission. The court finds out he's in violation, the judge'll issue a warrant for his arrest."

"Uh-huh. And he's already gone."

"Yeah. And it don't look like he's coming back for his trial, unless you find him and get him back here in time."

"Does his lawyer know he skipped?"

"Sam Wasserman? Hell, no. And he won't find out if we can help it."

That was easy enough to understand. Wasserman was a well-respected criminal attorney, but something of a straight arrow in a profession full of crooked bows. If he knew his client had skipped, he'd probably inform the court and then withdraw from the case.

"How long has your brother been gone, Ms. Beckett?" I asked.

"At least three days," she said. She had one of these soft, caressing voices, maybe natural, maybe affected. Intimate even when she was playing the worried little sister. "I had some business out of town and when I got back, he was gone from the apartment we share."

"What did he take with him?"

"Clothing, a few personal belongings."

"Cell phone?"

"Yes, but he has it turned off. I've left a dozen messages."

"Why do you think he ran away? At this particular time, I mean."

"The strain must have gotten to him... I shouldn't have left him alone. He's not a strong person and he's terrified of being locked up for a crime he didn't commit."

With any other client, Melikian would have rolled his eyes at that. Nine out of every ten bonds he posted was for an innocent party, to hear them and whoever arranged their bail tell it.

I said, "You have no idea where he might have gone?"

"None. Except that it won't be far, and there'll be a yacht harbor or marina or some kind of boat place nearby."

"Why do you say that?"

"Kenny hates traveling alone, any kind of travel. He won't fly and he's never driven more than a hundred miles in any direction by himself. And boats...they're his entire life."

"Working around them, you mean?"

"That's what he does—deckhand, maintenance man, any job that involves boats."

"Has he ever been in trouble with the law before?"

"No. Never."

So the travel restrictions didn't necessarily apply. Fear of prison can prod a man to do any number of things he'd shied away from before.

"The grand theft charge," I said. "What's he alleged to have stolen?"

"A diamond necklace. But he didn't steal it. I *know* he didn't."

That meant nothing, either. Most people refuse to believe a close relative capable of committing a major crime, no matter how much evidence exists to the contrary.

"How much is the necklace worth?"

"Assessed at twenty-K," Melikian said.

Some piece of jewelry. I asked who the owner was.

"Margaret Vorhees."

"Vorhees. Related to Andrew Vorhees?"

"His wife," Cory Beckett said. "His drunken, lying wife."

Andrew Vorhees was a big fish in the not-so-small San Francisco pond. High-powered union leader, ex-supervisor, yachtsman. A man with a reputation for high living and double-dealing, and a penchant for scandal. It was whispered around that he had kinky sexual tastes, had been a regular customer of one of the city's high-profile madams whose extensive call-girl operation the cops had busted a couple of years back. It was also whispered that his socialite wife was a severe alcoholic. She had cause, if the rumors about Vorhees were true.

"How does your brother know Margaret Vorhees?" I asked.

"He doesn't, not really. He works… worked for her husband."

"In what capacity?"

"Caring for his yacht. At the St. Francis Yacht Harbor."

"Is that where the theft occurred?"

"She claimed it was, yes…the Vorhees woman. From her purse while she was on the yacht."

"She carried a twenty-thousand-dollar necklace in her purse?"

"Taking it to a jeweler to have the clasp repaired, so she said. My brother was the only person on board at the time."

"Where was the necklace found?"

Cory Beckett sighed, flicked a lock of the midnight hair off her forehead. "Hidden inside Kenny's van."

I didn't say anything.

"He swears he didn't steal it, has no idea how it got into his van. Of course I believe him. He's not a thief. He had no possible reason to steal that necklace."

"Twenty-thousand dollars is a lot of temptation."

"Not to Kenny. He doesn't care about money. And he certainly wouldn't have taken it to give to me, as Margaret Vorhees claims. No, she put the necklace in his van, or had somebody do it for her."

"Why would she want to frame your brother?"

"I don't know. Neither does he. Some imagined slight, I suppose. Rich alcoholics...well, I'm sure you know how erratic and unpredictable people like that can be."

"Is your brother the kind of man who makes passes at married women?"

"Kenny? My God, no. What kind of question is that?"

"Sorry, but it's the kind I have to ask."

"He's not like that at all. He's a very shy person, especially around women. His only real problem...well..."

"Yes, Ms. Beckett?"

She ran the tip of her tongue back and forth along her lips, moistening them. The movement made Melikian squirm a little in his chair. "If I tell you," she said, "you'll think he's guilty, that he stole the necklace because of it."

"My job is to find him, not judge him."

"…All right. It's drugs."

"What kind of drugs?"

"Amphetamines."

"How bad is his habit?"

"It's not a habit, really. He only uses them when he's stressed out. But they don't help, they just make him paranoid, even delusional sometimes."

"Violent?"

"No. Oh, no. Never."

"Do you know who his supplier is?"

"No idea. I don't take drugs."

I hadn't suggested she did. That kind of quick defensive response is sometimes an indication of guilt, but then it was none of my business if she snorted coke five times a day and had a Baggie of the stuff in her purse. No judgments applied to her as well as her brother. Or so I thought then.

I said, "How much money did he take with him, do you know?"

"It couldn't be much more than a hundred dollars. Wherever he's gone, he'll try to get some kind of work connected with boats. That's the way he is."

"Does he have access to any of your bank accounts?"

"No. We keep our finances separate."

"Credit cards?"

"I let him use mine sometimes, but... no, none of his own."

"You said he drives a van. Make, model, color?"

"A Dodge Ram, dark blue. The right rear panel has a dent and a long scrape—a parking lot accident."

"Do you have the license number?"

She did and I wrote it down.

"Anything else you can tell me that might help me find him? Friends in the area, someone he might turn to for help?"

"There's no one like that. He doesn't make friends easily." She shifted position in the chair, re-crossed her legs the other way. Gnawed on her lip a little before she said, "Do you honestly think you can find him?"

"Sure he can," Melikian said. "He's the best, him and his people."

She said, "I don't care what you have to do or what it costs."

Abe winced at that, but he didn't say anything.

"No guarantees, of course," I said. "But if you're right that he's still somewhere in this general area, the chances are reasonably good."

"The one thing I ask," she said, "is that you let me know the minute you locate him. Don't try to talk him into coming back, don't talk to him at all if it can be avoided. Let me do it. I'm the only one he'll listen to."

"Fair enough. You understand, though, that if he refuses to return voluntarily, there's nothing we can do to force him."

Melikian said, "She understands. I explained it to her."

"And that we'd be bound to report his whereabouts to the authorities."

She nodded, and Abe said, "Do it myself in that case," without looking at her.

He wouldn't sacrifice even a small portion of $100,000 to keep his own mother out of jail.

I asked Cory Beckett for a photograph of her brother, and she produced a five-by-seven color snapshot from a big leather purse: Kenneth Beckett standing alone in front of a sleek ocean-going yacht. You could tell he and Cory were siblings—same black hair, though his was lank; same facial bone structure and wiry build—but where she was somebody you'd notice in a crowd, he was the polar opposite. Presentable enough, but there was nothing memorable about him. Just a kid in his early twenties, like thousands of others. The kind of individual you could spend an afternoon with, and five minutes after parting you'd have already forgotten what he looked like.

We got the paperwork out of the way and Cory Beckett wrote me a check for her half of the retainer; we'd bill Melikian for his half. The check had her address and phone number on it. The apartment she shared with her brother was on Nob Hill, a very expensive area of the city. Melikian had told me she worked as a model. One of the more successful variety, apparently.

We shook hands. Hers lingered in mine a little too long, I thought—and she favored me with another of her concerned little smiles while Melikian patted her shoulder and chewed on her with his eyes, and that was that. Routine interview. Routine skip-trace. Nothing special at all, except that for a change the client was a piece of eye candy.

Just goes to show how wrong first impressions can be.

3.

Back at the agency in South Park, I put the notes I'd made in order and gave them to Tamara to transcribe into a case file. She does most of the agency's computer work—I can operate one of the things, but not very well and not without a certain reluctance—and she's an expert. She also runs the business—coordinates the various investigations, handles billing and financial matters. My partner, Tamara Corbin: a twenty-eight-year-old desk jockey dynamo. She'd tripled our business since the partnership arrangement, to the point where we now employed two full-time field operatives, Jake Runyon and Alex Chavez, and had to bring in temps from time to time to handle the overload.

Tamara set to work on the preliminaries. Skip-traces are an essential part of the agency's business, along with insurance-related investigations and employee and personal background checks, and most can be dealt with by relying on the various real-time and other search engines we subscribe to. The Beckett case didn't seem to be one of them because of the circumstances, but you never know what might turn up on an Internet background search.

A little while later she came into my office from hers through the open connecting door, carrying a printout in one purple-nailed hand. The purple polish didn't go very well with her dark brown skin, or at least I didn't think it did, but I hadn't said anything to her about it and wouldn't. Who was I to criticize the fashion trends of a woman young enough to be my granddaughter?

"Nothing much on Kenneth Beckett," she said. "No record prior to the grand theft charge, just a couple of minor moving violations and a bunch of parking tickets, most of them in the L.A. area. Worked at two yacht harbors down there, Marina del Rey and Newport Beach. Good employment records in both places, left both jobs voluntarily for unspecified reasons. Worked on Andrew Vorhees' yacht for six months before his arrest, no problems there, either. Parents both dead, no family except the sister. No traceable contacts with anybody else down south or up here."

"Pretty much confirms what Cory Beckett told me about him."

"Yeah. But I'll bet she didn't tell you anything about *her* background. Juicy stuff."

"What, you checking up on our clients now, too?"

"Couldn't help it, close as her and her brother are." Tamara waggled the printout. "Kenny may be a nerd, but she's anything but. Some real interesting facts here."

"Such as?"

"For one, she's not a model. Not now, not ever."

"No? Then what does she do for a living?"

"Marries rich dudes. Two of 'em so far."

Well, that wasn't much of a surprise. "Married now? She wasn't wearing a wedding ring."

"Nope. First husband divorced her after eight months. She got enough of a settlement to set her up pretty sweet for a while. Number two lasted a little over a year. No divorce there, though."

"No?"

"Guy killed himself."

"Oh? For what reason?"

"Financial setbacks, according to the note he left," Tamara said. "But there's more to it than that. Two grown sons from a previous marriage claimed she was responsible for him offing himself."

"On what grounds?"

"Several. Two substantiated affairs during the year of marriage. Quote, bizarre sexual practices detrimental to his mental health, unquote."

"Bizarre?"

"Not a matter of public record what they were. Could be anything from orgies to goats to whips and chains."

"Goats?"

Tamara chuckled. One of her less than endearing traits is using her off the wall sense of humor to shock my old-fashioned sensibilities. "Sons also claimed she mishandled finances, and coerced him into making a new will that cut them out of the estate and left everything to her. They sued and had enough chops to get a favorable ruling. They got the big slice, she got a little one. Case brought her some negative publicity—probably one of the reasons she moved up here."

"So she's a promiscuous gold-digger. What does that have to do with her missing brother?"

"Nothing, maybe. Except that both her exes owned yachts berthed at local marinas, the first one in Marina del Rey, the second in Newport Beach."

I chewed on that for a bit. "So maybe it was the husbands who got Kenneth Beckett his jobs there."

"Uh-uh. He was working at both places before she hooked up with either guy."

"Well? Maybe she likes boats, too, hangs around where her brother works, and that's how she met the future husbands."

"Or he set up the meetings for her."

"What're you suggesting? The two of them working a scam to find her marriage partners?"

"Could be. He trolls around, finds a likely prospect, baits the hook, and she does the rest."

"Immoral, if so, but not illegal."

"No, but if that's the game, neither one of 'em's as innocent as she pretended to you."

"Clients have lied to us before," I said. "We don't have to like them or believe them as long as the lies have no bearing on the job we're hired to do. Besides, Abe Melikian's footing half the bill and we know he's all right."

Tamara said cynically, "Good thing for him he's not a rich yachtsman," and retreated into her office.

She compiled a list of all the yacht harbors and marinas in the greater Bay Area—

quite a few within a seventy-five-mile radius. Then she and I called the ones large enough to have full-time staff members who could check their records for recent hires. No Kenneth Beckett or anyone answering his description. Finding him wasn't going to be that easy. If he was working at all, it could be for a private party rather than as a marina or boatyard employee.

So it was going to take legwork, possibly a lot of it, to track him down. I used to handle much of the field jobs myself, but it got to be too much for a man pushing sixty-five. So did the five-day, sometimes six-day, grind. Now, after my decision a couple of years ago to semi-retire, I put in an average of two days a week at the office and only occasionally take on a field investigation. Hunting for Kenneth Beckett wouldn't be one of those occasions. Likely it would require piling up a lot of highway miles, asking the same questions and showing Beckett's photograph over and over again—pretty dull work.

Not for Jake Runyon, though. He thrived on that kind of assignment. Liked being out on the road, moving from place to place. Worked best when he could set his own schedule, his own pace.

Good man, Jake, a former Seattle cop and former investigator for one of the larger private agencies in the Pacific Northwest. Big, slab-faced, hammer-jawed. Smart, tough, loyal, and as honest as they come. He'd moved to San Francisco after the cancer death of his second wife, to try to reestablish a bond with an estranged son from his first marriage, the only family he had left. That hadn't worked out; he and Joshua were still estranged.

Runyon had been something of a reticent loner, still grieving for his dead wife, the first year or so he was with us. He'd come out of his shell somewhat since then, thanks in part to a hook-up with a woman named Bryn Darby, but he was still a hard man to get close to. Our relationship was mainly professional; we didn't socialize, probably never would. But we got along well, and more importantly, we had each other's backs. I'd trust him with my life—had, in fact, on more than one occasion.

Tamara and I were just finishing up when Runyon reported in. She gave him the Beckett case file, and after he'd looked it over he asked, "Priority job?"

"Pretty much," I said. "Beckett's trial is only ten days off."

"Okay. I'm on it."

4.

Jake Runyon

It looked like a fairly routine case to him, too, at first, if one with a certain amount of urgency. He'd handled dozens like it over the years—skip-traces, bail jumpers, missing persons—and with less information than he had to go on here. Assuming the sister was right about Kenneth Beckett's habit patterns, the odds were pretty good that he could be located before the trial date. Beckett didn't sound either mature or overly bright, which made him a poor candidate for grounding himself without leaving a traceable trail.

There were quite a few marinas and boatyards on Tamara's list. But Runyon figured he could eliminate the ones in close proximity to the city—Oakland, Alameda, Sausalito, Pacifica, the near end of the Peninsula. Even a half-smart, short-tether runaway would want a hiding place at some distance from his home turf. The remaining possibilities within a seventy-five mile radius could be covered by one man in the allotted time, though if Runyon didn't get a line on the subject by Day Five, Tamara said she'd assign Alex Chavez to help out.

Runyon started in Half Moon Bay, moved from there to the mid-Peninsula area, then down to San Jose and the rest of the south Bay. No luck. Stockton, Antioch, Rio Vista, Martinez, Suisun City, Vallejo. No luck. The North Bay next, starting with Sausalito, even though it was just across the Golden Gate Bridge, because of the town's large number of boating facilities. Another blank there. And one more in San Rafael.

On up to Port Sonoma. And that was where, on the morning of the fifth day, he finally got his fix on the subject's whereabouts.

The Port Sonoma marina was located in a wetlands area along the Petaluma River, near where it emptied into San Pablo Bay. Good-sized place with a ferry landing, a fuel dock and pump-out station, bait shop on one of the floats, and several rows of boat slips. The craft berthed in the slips were all sailboats and small inboards—no big yachts.

The day was a warmish, windy spring Saturday, and the marina was doing a brisk business—individuals and groups getting their craft ready to join those that already dotted the bay and the winding upland course of the river. Runyon went first to the bait shop, but nobody there recognized the photo of Kenneth Beckett. Same at the fuel dock. He walked down through an open gate to the slips. The first half-dozen people he buttonholed had nothing to tell him; the seventh, a lean, sun-bleached man in his mid-fifties working on the deck of a Sea Ray Sundancer, was the one who did.

The boat owner took a long look at the photo before he said, "Yeah, I've seen this kid. How come you're looking for him? He do something he shouldn't have?"

"Yes, and he'll be in a lot more trouble if I don't find him soon. When did you see him?"

"Last week. Seven, eight days ago."

"Here?"

"Right. Looking for work, he said. Seemed to know boats pretty well. But nobody's hiring, so I told him to check up at Belardi's."

"Where's that?"

"Upriver seven or eight miles."

"What kind of place?"

"Wide spot in the river—sandwich and bait shop, a few slips, some old fishing shacks. I heard the owner, old man Belardi, was looking for a handyman to fix up the rundown pier they got there."

"How do I get to Belardi's by car?"

"Easy. Go east on the highway, turn left at the first stoplight—Lakeville Highway. Seven or eight miles, like I said. Can't miss their sign."

Belardi's turned out to be one of those little enclaves that look as if they've been bypassed by time and progress. The restaurant and bait shop, the pier and a sagging boathouse, the handful of slips, the scattering of small houses and even smaller fishing shacks nearby all had a weathered, colorless look, like buildings in a black and white fifties movie. The Petaluma River, a saltwater estuary that had been granted river status so federal funds could be used to keep it dredged for boat traffic, was a couple of hundred yards wide at this point, its far side a long, wide stretch of tule marsh threaded with narrow waterways. More tule grass choked the shoreline on this side.

Several cars were parked in the gravel lot in front, none of them a dark blue Dodge van. Runyon crossed past the restaurant to a set of rickety stairs that led down to another gravel area, this one used as a combination boat repair and storage yard. From the stairs he could see that some recent work had been done on the short, shaky-looking pier that extended out to the slips. Two men were onboard an old sport-fisherman, one of five boats moored there; another man was just climbing up onto the pier from the float between the slips. None was Kenneth Beckett.

Runyon braced the man on the pier first, got a couple of negative grunts for the effort. The two on the sportfisherman didn't recognize the subject's photo, either, but one of them said, "Talk to old man Belardi, inside. Maybe he can help you."

Old man Belardi was an overweight seventy or so, cheerful until Runyon showed him the snapshot; then his round face turned mournful. "Don't tell me you're a cop."

Runyon said, "Private investigator," and proved it with the photostat of his license.

"Well, crap," Belardi said. "I get somebody I can rely on, hard worker, don't give me no trouble, and now you're gonna tell me he's a thief or molester or some damn thing."

"Not exactly. You did hire him, then?"

"Yeah, I hired him. Minimum wage and a place to stay. Seemed like a good kid, hard worker like I said—"

"A place to stay. Where?"

"Here. One of the river shacks."

"Which one?"

"Last up north."

"He there now, would you know?"

"If his van's there, he's there. I don't pay him to work weekends. Too much business, good weather like this."

Runyon nodded his thanks and started away.

"Hold on a minute," Belardi said. "What you gonna do? Haul him off to jail or something? Leave me with nobody to finish his work?"

"He'll be going back to the city, one way or another."

"I'm too old to make those repairs myself. I don't suppose you could hold off a few days, let him get the heavy work done?"

"No. Not possible."

Belardi sighed. "No damn luck, me or the kid."

5.
Jake Runyon

A paved driveway led downhill to the boat-yard, and a rutted, weed-choked track from there along the river to where the shacks squatted on the marshy ground. They were small, board-and-batten structures of one or maybe two rooms that must have been there for half a century or more; a short, stubby dock leaned out into the muddy water in front of each. There was no sign of life at the first two. The third also appeared deserted until Runyon rolled up in front; then he could see the van pulled in close to its far side wall—Dodge, dark blue, with a crumpled rear panel.

The sister's instructions were to notify her as soon as Beckett was found, without contact with the subject, but Runyon was too thorough a professional to act prematurely. He'd make sure Beckett was here, and that he would stay put, before reporting in.

He pulled up an angle so the nose of his Ford blocked the van, got out into a stiff breeze that carried the briny scent of the river and marshland. A long row of motionless blackbirds sat on a power line stretched out across the tules from Lakeville Highway, like a still from the Hitchcock movie. Somewhere upriver, an approaching powerboat laid a faint whine on the silence.

Runyon followed a tramped-down path through the grass to the door. A series of knocks brought no response. He tried the knob, found it unlocked. Pushed on it until it opened far enough, creaking a little, to give him a clear look inside.

Half of the riverfront wall was an uncurtained sliding-glass door; it let in enough light so that he could see a table, two chairs, a standing cabinet, a countertop with a hotplate, and a cot pushed in against the side wall. Kenneth Beckett lay prone on the cot, unmoving under a blanket, one cheek turned toward the door and draped with lank black hair half again as long as it had been when the snapshot was taken. The one visible eye was shut.

The only way for Runyon to tell if he was breathing or not was to go in and check. He did that. Breathing, yeah, in a fluttery kind of way—stoned, maybe. There was no visible evidence of drugs or drug paraphernalia in the room, but that didn't mean there wasn't any.

Leave him be, make his call? What he should've done, probably, but instinct dictated otherwise. He shook Beckett's shoulder, kept shaking it until the kid moaned and tried to pull away. Runyon got a grip on him, turned him over on his back. That woke him up.

He stared up at Runyon through pale blue eyes that took several seconds to focus and then filled with scare. He said thickly, "Who're you? I don't know you…"

"My name is Runyon, Jake Runyon. I'm here to help you."

"Help me? I don't need any help…"

Beckett struggled to sit up. Runyon let him do that, but held him with a tight hand on his shoulder when he tried to lift himself off the cot. The left side of his face began a spasmodic twitching.

"You high on something, Ken?"

"What? No! I don't use drugs—" Beckett's body jerked suddenly, as if he'd been touched by a live wire. His mouth bent into a crooked line. "Oh Jesus! She told you that, didn't she? *She* sent you!"

"If you mean your sister—"

"Another one, a *new* one."

"You're not making sense—"

Without warning Beckett lunged upward, tearing loose from Runyon's grip, slammed a shoulder into him and streaked for the door. There was surprising strength in the kid's wiry body; the blow sent Runyon reeling sideways into the table, barking his shin and almost taking him off his feet. By the time he recovered Beckett was through the door.

Runyon hobbled out after him, spotted him running for his van. But Beckett pulled up when he saw the Ford blocking escape, stood indecisive for a couple of seconds, then ran past the van toward the river's edge. Halfway there, his feet slid out from under him and he went tumbling through the tule grass.

Runyon caught up to him just as he dragged himself upright, spun him around. He had forty pounds on the kid, plus years of judo training when he was on the Seattle PD; Beckett struggled in his grasp, couldn't break free this time, finally quit struggling when Runyon said sharply, "Quit it! Stand still! You're not going anywhere until we talk."

Beckett stood with his eyes downcast, his breath coming in short, quick pants. "I don't want to talk to you."

"But you're going to. Inside. No argument."

Runyon led him back to the shack, one hand tight on his arm. He shut the door behind them, walked Beckett to the cot and sat him down on it again.

"You calm enough now to listen to me?"

"Why can't she leave me alone?" Beckett muttered. "Why can't everybody just leave me alone?"

"Listen, I said. I'm not involved with your sister, I've never even met her. I'm a private investigator—the agency I work for was hired to find you. You understand?"

"Investigator?" As if the word didn't quite compute. "You mean...Cory hired you?"

"Her and your bail bondsman."

Beckett drew a long, shuddery breath. "I won't go to prison for something I didn't do, not for her, not for anybody."

"If you don't show up for your trial, you'll go to prison whether you're innocent or not. You're already in violation of your bail terms."

"You can't make me go back."

"That's right," Runyon said. "But if you don't go voluntarily, we're required by law to report the violation and the judge'll issue an arrest warrant. Is that what you want?"

The kid stared off into space, his eyes bright with misery. After a time he said thickly, "It's Cory's fault, not mine. None of this'd be happening if I hadn't let her talk me into it."

"Into what?"

Headshake. Runyon repeated the question twice more before he got a low-voiced response.

"Taking the blame."

"The blame. For the crime you're charged with?"

"Pretending it was me she was out to get."

"Who? Cory?"

"Mrs. Vorhees."

Runyon backed away from the cot, took one of the chairs and straddled it. "Let's get this straight. Did you steal Margaret Vorhees' necklace?"

"No. Nobody stole it."

"Then how did it get into your van?"

"Chaleen put it there. She told him to."

"Mrs. Vorhees?"

"No, no. Cory."

"Why would your sister do that to you?"

Headshake.

Runyon asked, "Who's Chaleen?"

"That bastard. She's fucking him, too."

Trying to make sense of what Beckett was saying was like riding on a fast-moving carousel. Round and round, round and round. "Where did Chaleen get the necklace?"

"From Mrs. Vorhees. She wanted him to hide it in Cory's car so it'd look like she stole it."

"How could Cory be blamed if you were the only other person on the boat that day?"

"I wasn't. She was there when Mrs. Vorhees showed up."

"To see you, you mean?"

"No. Mr. Vorhees. She... No, I'm not supposed to talk about that."

"Who told you not to? Cory?"

Headshake.

"All right. So your sister was the intended target, but she talked Chaleen into framing you instead. That what you're saying?"

"Yes. She can make anybody do anything she wants. Anybody. Anything."

"Why would Mrs. Vorhees want to frame your sister?"

"She hates Cory."

"Why?"

Headshake.

"When did Cory tell you that you had to take the blame? Before or after Chaleen planted the necklace in your van?"

"Before."

"And you just let it happen?"

"I told you, she always gets what she wants."

"That doesn't answer my question."

"She said we had to, we couldn't rock the boat."

"What boat?"

Beckett said in a mimicking falsetto, "'Trust me, Kenny. Don't I always know what's best for you, me, our future. I'll make sure you don't go to prison.'" He seemed close to tears now. "She doesn't care about me as much as she says she does. The only person she really cares about is herself. Ever since she hooked up with that goddamn Hutchinson…"

"Hutchinson. Who's he?"

Headshake.

Ramblings. Yet as improbable and inconsistent as Beckett's story sounded, it didn't strike Runyon as lies, delusions, or drug-induced fantasy. The kid was an emotional weakling strung out on fear, not a chemical substance. Fear of his sister, it seemed, as much of being sent to prison.

Runyon said, "Anything more you want to tell me?"

"No. I shouldn't have...I...no."

"So what's it going to be? Back to San Francisco voluntarily, or do I notify the authorities?"

A rapid series of headshakes this time. "I want to stay here. I like it here."

"You can't do that. It's either your apartment or a jail cell and an unlawful flight charge. Be smart. Let me take you back."

"No."

"Then let your sister come and get you—"

"No!"

"If you don't go with me, I'll have to tell her where you are."

Beckett flattened himself face down on the cot again, yanked the blanket up to his neck. "No more talking…my head hurts, I can't think. Go away, leave me alone."

"Ken—"

"Go away!" Another jerk on the blanket, so that it covered his head. Burying himself under it. "Go away, go away, *go away*!"

Runyon had no choice now. He went outside to call the agency.

6.

I seldom work on Saturdays, but I had a couple of hours of leftover business to attend to and Kerry and Emily had made mother-daughter plans that didn't include me, so I was at my desk when Runyon checked in. Tamara was at hers, too; she'd gone through a recent spate of personal troubles and was coping with them, or not coping with them, by being a workaholic.

Good news that Jake had found Kenneth Beckett, but the details of their conversation didn't set any better with me than they did with him. Runyon's instincts were pretty well honed; if he believed Beckett's story was straight goods, then likely it was. Which made Cory Beckett the complete opposite of what she'd seemed in Abe Melikian's office. Control freak, sex addict, liar, schemer. With motives that didn't seem to make much sense. How could Kenneth

Beckett taking the fall on a bogus theft charge benefit either of them?

I'd told Tamara that it didn't matter if a client lied to us, and that was true enough up to a point. But if the lies and misrepresentations involved a felony, we had a duty not to ignore them.

"You haven't notified the client yet?" I asked.

Runyon said, "No. I thought I'd give Beckett a few minutes to calm down, then make one more try at reasoning with him."

"Likely to do any good?"

"I doubt it. He's pretty strung out."

"But not on drugs."

"No."

"So that's a confirmed lie. Cory didn't want us talking to him, but in case we did, we'd put down anything he said to junkie ravings."

"Same take here."

"Okay. Let me break the news to her, see if I can find out what she's up to. If you can convince Beckett to let you bring him back, go ahead. But deliver him here to the office, not to their apartment."

"Right."

"Let me know if that's how it plays out. Otherwise, hang around the shack and keep an eye on him until you hear from me."

"He's not going anywhere," Runyon said. "I've got his van blocked with my car and I'll take his keys to make sure."

After we rang off, I went in to brief Tamara. She said, "Weird. What d'you think the Beckett woman's up to?"

"No idea…yet."

"How about I do a deep backgrounder on her? That stuff I pulled up the last week only scratched the surface."

"Go ahead when you have the time."

"Like right now."

7.

The Beckett apartment on Nob Hill was only ten minutes or so from South Park, but street parking up there is difficult and garage parking fees exorbitant. It took me another ten minutes to find curb space, one that was only marginally legal and two steep uphill blocks away. I was short of breath by the time I reached the building, a venerable four-story pile near Huntington Park that may or may not have been some fat cat's private mansion a hundred years ago. Nob Hill, or Snob Hill as the locals sometimes call it, is where many of the city's upper class families and affluent Yuppies hang their hats. It takes big bucks to live there, and I found myself wondering if Cory Beckett had dragged enough out of her two marriages to pay the rent, or if somebody else—not her deckhand brother—was contributing to the monthly nut.

Somebody named Andrew Vorhees.

I had that confirmed a lot quicker than I could have expected. About ten seconds after I reached the building, as a matter of fact. Just as I stepped into the vestibule, the entrance door opened and a man came striding out. His glance at me as he passed by was brief and dismissive; I was nobody he knew.

But I'd seen his picture and I knew him: Andrew Vorhees.

I managed to catch the pneumatic door just before it latched, slipped inside as Vorhees turned out of the vestibule. So what had he been doing here? Something to do with his former employee and the theft charge? More likely, he'd been visiting Cory Beckett for personal reasons—the same personal reasons, if Kenneth Beckett's story was true, she'd been visiting Vorhees on his yacht the day of the alleged theft. Nice conquest for a scheming woman, a man in the same wealthy yachtsman class as her two ex-husbands. The fact that he was married wouldn't mean much to a playboy with his reputation, but it might mean plenty to his wife. If Vorhees was having an affair with Cory Beckett, it was a possible explanation for the aborted attempt to frame her.

The Beckett apartment was number 8, top floor front. I rode the elevator up, pushed a pearl bell button. There was a one-way peephole in the door, but Cory Beckett didn't bother to look through it. The door opened almost immediately, wide enough so I could see she was wearing a shimmery lavender silk negligee at one o'clock in the afternoon, and she said, "Did you forget—" before she saw me standing there.

You had to give her credit: her caught-off-guard reaction lasted no more than a couple of seconds. The rounded O of her mouth reshaped into a tentative smile, her body relaxed, and she was back in control.

"Oh," she said, "hello. How did you—?"

"Get in without using the intercom? Andrew Vorhees."

Didn't faze her at all. "I'm sorry?"

"He was leaving the building just as I arrived."

"What would Andrew Vorhees be doing here?"

"Just what I was wondering. Pretty unlikely coincidence that he'd be visiting somebody else who lives in this building."

She said, not quite challengingly, "And if it was me? It's really none of your business, is it?" Pause. "Why are *you* here? Do you have news about Kenny?"

She was good, all right. Stonewall, skirt the issue, then a quick shift of subject. I let her get away with it for the time being.

"News, yes," I said.

"You've found him? Where is he?"

"Why don't we talk inside, Ms. Beckett? If you don't mind."

"Yes, of course. Come in."

It was like walking into an abstract art exhibit. Each wall painted a different primary color, gaudy paintings and hangings, multi-hued chairs and couches, half a dozen gold-flecked mirrors in different shapes and sizes that magnified the riotous color scheme. The place made me uncomfortable, but it also gave me an insight into

Cory Beckett. The cool, low-key exterior was pure façade; inside she was like the living space she'd created, a mind full of flash and intensity and controlled chaos. Her emotional, weak-willed brother must hate this place, I thought. So why did he live here with her? Why did she want him to?

After she closed the door she made a vague apologetic gesture with one hand, the other holding the top of the negligee closed at her throat. "I'm sorry I'm not dressed. I haven't been feeling well…" Quick change of subject again. "Kenny. You *have* found him?"

"One of our operatives has, yes."

"Is he all right?"

"More or less."

"Where is he?"

"Before I tell you, I have some questions."

"Questions? I don't understand."

"About the lies you told in Abe Melikian's office."

"I don't… Lies?" Injured innocence, now. "I don't have any idea what you mean."

"I think you do. Your brother's alleged drug use, for one. He's not into drugs at all."

"Of course he is, sometimes. Why would you think otherwise?"

"His word. And no illegal substance of any kind where he's living."

"His word? You spoke to him?"

"The operative, Jake Runyon, did. Judgment call on his part."

"Then...Mr. Runyon's bringing him home?"

"No. Your brother refuses to leave with him. Seems he's not too keen on seeing you again, either."

"Oh God, I was afraid of this. That's why I asked you not to talk to him, to let me handle him."

"His version of the theft business is nothing like yours," I said. "He claims the necklace was supposed to be planted in your car, not his van, by a man named Chaleen."

"What? Why would I be the intended victim?"

"Because Margaret Vorhees has cause to hate you, he said."

"That's ridiculous. I don't even know the woman."

"But you do know her husband."

"Not very well."

"Your brother says you were with Vorhees on his yacht that day."

"Did he? Well, I wasn't." She sighed in a put-upon way. "What else did Kenny say?"

"That you talked Chaleen into stashing the necklace in his van."

Shocked stare. "Why on earth would I do a thing like that?"

"Important to both your futures that he take the blame, he said. Keep from rocking the boat."

"That doesn't make any sense. How could your man Runyon believe such a wild story? Poor Kenny's not stable…couldn't he see that? Can't you?"

I didn't say anything.

"He imagines things," she said, "makes up stories that aren't true. What did he say about me? That I don't really care about him, that I force him to do things against his will? That I'm a bad person? Well, I'm not. He's my brother and I love him, I only want what's best for him—"

"Who's Chaleen, Ms. Beckett?"

"I don't have any idea." She gnawed at her lower lip for a couple of seconds, then in a tentative way walked over to where I stood. Close enough so I could smell the musky perfume she was wearing. Close enough for those luminous eyes of hers to probe intently into mine. "I'm sorry you think badly of me," she said then, "but please, just tell me where Kenny is so I can bring him home."

Nice little performance, but I wasn't fooled by it or affected by her scent or the nearness of her. Vamp stuff doesn't work on me; I've been around too long, seen too much.

I said, "He's at a place called Belardi's on the Petaluma River, about forty miles north of here. Third of three fishing shacks on the north side of the pier. Runyon's there keeping an eye on him."

"Thank you." She held eye contact a few seconds more; then, when I still didn't respond, she produced another of her little smiles and slowly backed off. "Now if you'll please leave so I can get dressed…"

I left. It had been an unsatisfactory interview, but Cory Beckett wasn't easily rattled—practiced liars usually aren't—and I'd prodded her as far as I dared.

8.

Jake Runyon

It was almost three o'clock before Kenneth Beckett's sister showed up at Belardi's.

Nothing happened in the interim. Runyon went back inside the shack after he finished the phone conversation with Bill, to conduct a quick search for weapons and/or drugs. For all he knew Beckett was suicidal and the last thing he wanted was a dead man on his watch. He found nothing, not even a sharp knife. Just the keys to the van, which he pocketed. Beckett stayed buried under the blanket, sleeping or hiding.

Outside again, Runyon unlocked the van and poked around among the clutter of tools, paint cans, and other items. Nothing there, either, in the way of weapons or illegal substances.

Runyon did his waiting in the car. He was used to downtime and he dealt with it by putting himself into the equivalent of a computer's sleep mode—a trick he'd learned to help him get through the long months of Colleen's agonizingly slow death. Aware, ready for immediate action if necessary, but otherwise as shut down mentally as he was physically.

Boats passed up and down the river, a few of them stopping at the Belardi's dock; cars came and went. Nobody approached the shack until the newish, yellow-and-black Camaro came jouncing along the riverfront track and slid to a stop nearby.

Two occupants, the woman driving and a male passenger. Runyon got out when they did, so that the three of them came together in front of the shack. Cory Beckett was just as Bill had described her, sleek and slender in a white turtleneck sweater and designer jeans, her black hair swirling in the wind off the marshland. The animal magnetism she possessed was palpable enough, but Runyon would not have responded to it even if he hadn't had the conversation with Kenneth Beckett. Subtly sexy women attracted him; the too-cool, smolderingly seductive type left him cold.

She said, "Mr. Runyon? I'm Kenneth's sister, Cory. This is a friend I brought along to drive Kenny's van back to the city."

No introduction, just "a friend." The man nodded once but said nothing, made no offer to shake hands. He was in his mid-thirties, sandy-haired, well set up and pretty-boy handsome except for a quirk at one corner of his mouth that gave the impression of a perpetual lopsided sneer.

Runyon said, "Your brother's inside, Ms. Beckett."

"Is he rational? I mean, I understand you talked to him and he told you some wild stories that aren't true."

"Is he rational," not "is he all right." Seemed she was less worried about her brother's welfare than about what he might have revealed.

"Calm enough. Withdrawn."

"Tractable, then," she said. Tractable. Another less than concerned word. "That's a relief. He's not easy to handle when he's in one of his manic states."

Runyon had nothing to say to that.

"I'll get him," she said. "You don't need to wait any longer."

"I'll just make sure he goes along peaceably."

"She said you don't need to wait," the sandy-haired man said. "If Cory can't handle him, I can."

"I'll wait anyway."

Sandy-hair seemed to want to make an issue of it. The Beckett woman said, "It's all right, Frank," smiled at him the way you'd smile at an overly aggressive pet, put her smoky eyes on Runyon for three or four seconds, and then moved on past him to the door.

Runyon stood watching the shack. Frank paced back and forth on the weedy ground, his hands thrust into the pockets of a light jacket. The electrical wire strung in from the highway thrummed in the wind; that was the only sound until Kenneth Beckett let out a wailing cry from inside and began shouting, "No, no, I won't, why can't you leave me alone!"

Runyon started toward the shack, but Frank cut over in front of him and grabbed his arm. "Stay out of it," he said. "She can handle him."

"Let go of my arm."

"Yeah? Suppose I don't?"

Runyon jerked loose, started around the man. Combatively Frank moved to block him. They did a little two-step dance that ended with Frank trying to shove him backwards, saying, "Don't mess with me, man, I'll knock you on your ass—"

He half choked on the last word because by then Runyon, in two fast moves, had his arm locked down against his side with forearm and wrist grips. That brought them up tight against each other, their faces a couple of inches apart. Frank tried to struggle free, making growling noises in his throat, but Runyon held him immobile for half a dozen beats before he let go. When he stepped back, it was just far enough to set himself in case Frank had any more notions.

He didn't. Just glared and rubbed his arm without quite making eye contact again. Runyon had dealt with his type any number of times while on the Seattle PD and since. An assertive hard-nose until he came up against somebody harder, more assertive.

Runyon put a little more distance between them before he turned toward the shack. The yelling had stopped; it was quiet in there now. But he went to the door anyway, shoved it open.

The two of them, brother and sister, were standing next to the table, close enough for her to have been putting low-voiced words into his ear. Both looked at Runyon in the open doorway. Beckett's face was moist with sweat, but she'd managed to calm him down. He looked docile enough in a resigned, trapped way.

"It's all right, Mr. Runyon," Cory Beckett said. "He'll come with me now. Won't you, Kenny?"

He shook his head, but the word that came out of his mouth was "Yes."

She slid her arm around him. "I'll help you pack." Then, to Runyon, "We'll be ready in a few minutes. It's really all right for you to leave now."

No, it wasn't. He shut the door to give them privacy. Frank was moving around behind him, walking off his anger and humiliation in tight little pacing turns. Runyon went to the Ford, backed it up far enough to allow the van clearance, then switched off the engine and got out to stand next to the driver's door. He didn't move, watching Frank continue to pace, until the Becketts came out five minutes later.

Kenneth Beckett balked when he saw the sandy-haired man. "Why'd you have to bring *him*?" he said to his sister.

"I told you inside, Kenny. Somebody has to drive your van back to the city."

"Not him. I don't want him in my van."

"Would you rather ride with him than me?"

"No! Oh, Jesus, Cory—"

"Hush now. No more fuss."

Runyon moved over to where they stood. Cory Beckett said, "Why are you still here?"

"Because my job's not finished until you're on your way. And because I have the keys to the van."

He gave them to her. Frank came stomping over, took the keyring out of her hand. He said to Runyon through a sideways glare, "I hope we cross paths again sometime, man. Things'll be different then."

"I doubt that."

Frank stalked away to the van. Kenneth Beckett said to Runyon without looking at him, "I didn't mean what I said before. About my sister, about the necklace…I made it all up. I was disoriented. I didn't know what I was saying."

Runyon made no response. The words had a dull, recited cadence, like lines delivered by an amateur actor. Coached, he was thinking as Cory Beckett led her brother to the Camaro. Part of what she'd been whispering into the kid's ear inside the shack. It

made him all the more convinced that what
Beckett had told him earlier was the truth.

9.

Back at the agency, I gave Tamara a short rundown of my interview with Cory Beckett. The woman's apparent involvement with Andrew Vorhees didn't surprise her any more than it had me.

"Real piece of work, all right," she said. "Whatever she's up to, you can bet it's more than just being Vorhees' mistress."

"If she is his mistress."

"Oh yeah. Her name's on the lease for that Snob Hill apartment, but the monthly rent's sixty-five hundred. She came out of her marriages fairly well fixed, but not well enough to be living it up without some extra juice. Up until six months ago she and Kenny shared a place in Cow Hollow that rented for under three thousand."

"So you don't think she could have afforded Abe Melikian's ten thousand bond commission and whatever collateral she had to put up for the rest."

"The ten K, maybe, but what do you bet Vorhees supplied the collateral. There're blog rumors he's been keeping a woman on the side. Dude's not exactly what you'd call discreet."

"His wife must be a glutton for punishment," I said. "Otherwise, why not divorce instead of separation."

"Still loves the dude," Tamara said. "Either that, or she doesn't like to lose what belongs to her."

"And Vorhees doesn't dump her because?"

"He can't afford to. Take him right off the gravy train. He's got some money of his own, but what lets him own a yacht and live in St. Francis Wood is her money. Inherited. Big bucks."

"Uh-huh."

"So he stays for the money and screws around because he knows he can get away with it up to a point. Only he crossed some line with Cory Beckett that the missus wouldn't put up with. Spending too much on her, or getting too involved. Woman like Margaret Vorhees gets jealous enough, she's liable to do anything."

"Like framing a rival."

"Or having an affair of her own."

"Is that another blog rumor?"

"Yep."

"Sauce for the goose," I said.

"Huh?"

Sometimes I forget twenty-somethings can be unfamiliar with the old sayings codgers like me grew up on. "Never mind. What else does the blog rumor mill say?"

"This is where it gets juicy. Evidently the dude Mrs. Vorhees had the affair with was Frank Chaleen."

"Well, well. And just who is Chaleen?"

"A peanut vendor."

"A...what?"

"Owns a company that makes plastic packing material. You know, plastic peanuts. Chaleen Manufacturing, founded by his father. Had political ambitions for a while, got to know Andrew Vorhees when he was on the Board of Supes and worked with him on union negotiations. They had a big falling-out about five months ago. Almost started beating on each other in a downtown restaurant, so it made the blogs."

"Because Vorhees found out Chaleen was sleeping with his wife?"

"Yep. Okay for him to screw around as much as he wants, but he didn't like her doing it with one of his pals. Apparently he's the one who pushed for the separation, one of those on again, off again deals. Mostly he lives on the yacht, her in the Wood house."

I chewed on that for a time. Andrew Vorhees, Margaret Vorhees, Cory Beckett, and Frank Chaleen, all tied together in a not-so-neat little package. "Is Chaleen still seeing Mrs. Vorhees?"

"If he is, it's on the sly," Tamara said. "You thinking that's how she got him to help her frame Cory?"

"Could be. Might also explain why she hasn't tried something like it again."

"Only the frame didn't work on account of Cory's ten years younger than Margaret and has a lot more to offer in the bed department."

"Uh-huh. In which case Chaleen either initiated contact with Cory for that reason, or they were already seeing each other. Met through Vorhees, maybe."

"Must've pissed Cory off big time when she found out she was the target," Tamara said. "Kind of woman *she* is, she's not about to let her meal ticket go without a fight."

"So she jeopardizes her relationship with him by sleeping and conniving with Chaleen. Why? What kind of fight do you put up by letting your brother get framed instead of you? For that matter, why didn't she just let Vorhees handle the situation with his wife?"

"Maybe that's what not wanting to rock the boat means."

"Still doesn't explain all the scheming."

"Well, Kenny must know or suspect what she's up to. That's why she was so eager to have us find him—get him back home where she can keep an eye on him."

"Can't be the only reason," I said. "She has to have some feelings for him. Took care of him in southern California, lets him live with her here."

"Took care of him when he was a kid, too, after their mother died."

"Which makes her motives all the more inexplicable. She must want him to beat the theft charge, or she wouldn't have hired a high-powered lawyer to defend him."

"Kind of a mind fuck, all right," Tamara said.

I gave her a look, and she grinned and waggled an eyebrow. Old-fashioned workplace decorum defeated once more by the modern penchant for casual obscenity. "What else did you find out about the Becketts?"

"Nothing else on him. A few more eye-openers about her. For one, she got busted one night in L.A. when she was nineteen for lewd and lascivious behavior, soliciting, and contributing to the delinquency of a minor. Got caught with a kid from a rich family she did some nanny work for, fifteen years old, doing the nasty in a public park."

"Where does the soliciting charge come in?"

"Seems she told the kid she'd do it with him for two hundred bucks."

"Nice," I said sourly. "Disposition of the case?"

"Wasn't any. All charges dropped before she could be arraigned."

"How come?"

"The kid changed his story about who offered the two hundred, said it was him, not her. His old man refused to press the other two charges. So she got off with a wrist-slap fine."

"Why would the father step in that way?"

"Why do you think?" Tamara flashed another impish grin. "Not that there was any hard evidence to prove he was screwing her, too."

I let that pass. "She have any other trouble with the law?"

"One brush, about a year later. Got mixed up with an ex-con named Hutchinson. Ugly biker dude with weird-ass tattoos all over him—there's a photo on the Net. Had a list of burglary and robbery priors a foot long."

"Hutchinson. Beckett mentioned that name to Jake."

"Uh-huh. But he doesn't have anything to do with what's going on now."

"No? How do you know?"

"Dude's dead. Been dead six years. Shot and killed by the Riverside cops during commission of an armed robbery. Some suspicion Cory was mixed up in a couple of his other crimes right before that, but they couldn't prove it. So she walked."

Evidently Cory Beckett wasn't in the least discriminating when it came to men. Young, old, handsome, ugly, felons, yachtsmen, and Christ knew what other kind. The only constant seemed to be money— how much the individual had, how much she could get her hands on.

"What's her family background?" I asked.

"Grew up poor in a little town near Riverside," Tamara said. "Father split around the time Kenneth was born, mother worked as a house cleaner and died of an aneurism when Cory was sixteen and Kenny twelve. Kids lived with an aunt for two years, during which time Cory got herself thrown out of high school. No public record of why, but you can pretty much figure it had something with sex. Right around then she moved out on her own and took her brother with her."

"Supported them how?"

"Nanny jobs with rich folks. Screwing for money, too, probably. Made enough to move to Santa Monica. That was when Kenny started working the boating scene. A year after that, she climbed on the marriage-go-round."

"Pretty sorry resume."

"Say that again. So what do we do about her?"

"Not much we can do, unless Abe Melikian wants us to pursue the matter on his behalf."

"Doubt it. All he cares about is not losing his bond money."

"Then we'll have to drop it. You know we can't continue an investigation without a client."

"Yeah. Damn, though. I'd sure like to know what that woman's up to."

"So would I. After the fact with nobody hurt, and from a safe distance."

10.

Abe Melikian was another Saturday workaholic, in his office and busy with a client when I rang up. I told the staff member I spoke with to let him know I had news for him and would deliver it in person within the hour.

Runyon checked in just as I was leaving the agency. The sandy-haired man named Frank who'd showed up at Belardi's with Cory Beckett was Frank Chaleen; Tamara confirmed it from Jake's description. The woman was brazen as hell. Lied in her teeth to me about not knowing Chaleen, then as soon as I was gone, called him in to help her fetch her brother home.

Melikian, as Tamara had predicted, didn't want us to do any more investigating. He was upset that we'd probed as much as we had. He already knew that Kenneth Beckett had been found and Cory was bringing him back to keep his trial date because she'd called to tell him so, and why the hell hadn't I notified him right away myself instead of going to her apartment and harassing her?

I tried to explain about her background, her ties to Vorhees and Chaleen, the lies and manipulations we'd uncovered, but I might as well have been talking to a wall. He refused to consider that she might be anything other than the selfless sister she pretended to be; kept defending her and her intentions. Kenneth Beckett was unstable, he said, parroting what she'd told me; the kid's sudden run-out proved that. The story he'd told Runyon was "a load of drug-raving bullshit." Cory had her brother's best interests at heart, was doing everything she could to keep him out of prison, etc.

Old Abe was hooked, all right. So deeply hooked that I couldn't help wondering if she was sleeping with him, too. He was always paying lip service to family and family values—he'd been married thirty years, had two grown daughters and a son in high school—and I had taken him for a straight arrow. But when a sexy piece half a man's age makes herself available to him, the temptation for some can be too strong to resist. Not me, not with a woman like Cory Beckett—that's what I told myself. But how could I be absolutely sure I wouldn't succumb under the right, or wrong, circumstances?

I said, "Okay, Abe. Have it your way. We'll back off."

"Damn well better. Beckett's back, I'm not gonna lose my bond, case closed. You want any more business from me, stay the hell away from Cory and her brother."

So that's the end of it, I thought. Kenneth Beckett gets convicted or acquitted at his trial, his sister goes right on lying, manipulating, using men to her own ends, and we forget the whole sorry business and move on. Case closed.

Only it wasn't.

Not by a longshot.

11.
Jake Runyon

The call came a little before nine on Monday night, three days before Kenneth Beckett's trial was scheduled to start.

Runyon was home, or what passed for home—a drafty, one-bedroom apartment on Ortega Street, off Nineteenth Avenue. Doing what he usually did on the two or three evenings a week he wasn't with Bryn: watching an old movie on TV, as much for the noise as for the film itself. This one didn't interest him much, an old musical with Bing Crosby, the only thing on that didn't have laugh tracks, halfwits making fools of themselves in so-called reality shows, or macho types firing off automatic weapons, cars and buildings blowing up, and an excess of blood and gore. So he was only half paying attention, his mind cranked down, his body relaxed. Waiting for it to be late enough to go to bed.

It was his landline that rang, not his cell. He came close to not answering it. Landline calls at this time of night were usually either wrong numbers or telemarketers of one stripe or another. Not this time. He picked up on the sixth ring, mainly to shut off the clamor, and a man's scratchy voice, not familiar at first, said, "Mr. Runyon?"

"If you're selling me something—"

"No, no. No. I remembered your name, I looked in the phone book…"

"Kenneth Beckett?"

"Yes. I…need to talk to somebody. I don't know anyone else."

"Talk about what?"

"Cory. She…I can't let her…"

"Yes?"

Silence. Runyon was about to prompt him when Beckett said, "Not on the phone, okay? I can't talk about this on the phone."

"Are you home? I can come there—"

"No! Cory's out now, but she could be back any time."

"Meet me somewhere, then."

"I can't. She'll be just as mad if I'm not here when she gets back. She doesn't want me to go out by myself at night." Beckett's voice rose, turned querulous. "She took my car keys, my cell phone…I promised her I wouldn't run away again, but she doesn't believe me."

"Can you get out during the daytime?"

"I asked her if I could go down to the yacht club tomorrow. She said yes, but I have to take a bus. A fucking bus."

"Which yacht club?"

"Where I used to work. The St. Francis."

Runyon thought it over. He had a case interview scheduled in the morning, but it could be postponed. From the sound of Beckett's voice, whatever he had to say about his sister was more important. "Why don't I meet you there in the morning?"

"They won't let me in after what happened. Took that away from me, too. All I can do is stand outside and look in."

"Name a time and a place to meet. I'll be there."

"Just you? Nobody else?"

"Just me."

More silence. Then, "I have to be careful. If she finds out…"

"You can trust me. I don't betray confidences."

"Okay. You know the big green clock in front of the St. Francis, right by the parking lot?"

"I can find it."

Beckett said he'd be there at ten. Then he said as if to himself, "I have to do this, I *have* to," and broke the connection.

12.
Jake Runyon

Even on a weekday morning the Marina Green and the area along the West Harbor yacht basin was packed with joggers, women pushing baby strollers, adults and children on benches and grass taking advantage of the warming spring sun.

Runyon had driven down early because parking at the only part of the Green he'd been to before, near Gashouse Cove and Fort Mason, was at a premium and he'd figured the same might be true at the opposite end. Not so. There were plenty of spaces in the lot on Yacht Road near the St. Francis. So he had twenty minutes to kill until ten o'clock.

The big green clock Beckett had mentioned was easy to spot—a Roman-numeraled Rolex atop an old-fashioned standard a dozen feet tall, between the parking lot and

the tan, Spanish style yacht club. A rocky
seawall ran behind the club on the bay
side; stretched out in front was West Harbor where the club members' boats were
berthed, a thin forest of masts extending
out to Marina Boulevard. In that direction
you could see the Golden Gate Bridge and
the big sunlit dome of the Palace of Fine
Arts.

Runyon was too restless to stand waiting there for twenty minutes. He went the
other direction, through a break in the seawall and along a bayfront walkway. From
there, if you cared, you had a clear look at
the wide sweep of the bay where a few sailboats tacked along and a tourist boat was
headed toward Alcatraz. He paid little attention. Scenic views and panoramas didn't
interest him anymore; hadn't since Colleen's death. He noted landmarks to orient
himself or for future reference. Otherwise,
places were just places, colorless, void of
any distinction or attraction.

He got rid of fifteen minutes on the
bayfront walk. Beckett still hadn't showed

when he returned to the clock, so he crossed to the cement strip that ran along the harbor's upper edge. Wandered a short distance past sailboats, yachts, other large craft in their slips, then back again.

A little after ten, and Beckett still hadn't shown. Runyon went to do some more pacing around under the clock.

Five minutes, ten minutes. He was beginning to wonder if the kid had changed his mind when Beckett finally appeared, hurrying along the far edge of the boat basin. Not quite running but moving fast, head down, arms pumping like pistons.

Runyon moved to meet him at the top of the parking lot. He didn't look much better than he had at the shack at Belardi's. Pale, nervous, bagged and blood-flecked eyes indicating more than one sleepless night. The eyes held on Runyon's, flicked away, flicked back, flicked away.

"Sorry I'm late. She almost didn't let me go out today. I had to promise to be back by noon."

"Why is that?"

"Meeting with Mr. Wasserman, the lawyer, this afternoon. And dinner tonight with…" Beckett let the rest of it trail off. "Let's go over by the slips, okay?"

Runyon followed him to the walkway, where Beckett leaned on the iron railing above the slips. At intervals, ramps led down to locked gates that barred public access to the moored craft. Beckett gestured at the nearest gate and said in hurt tones, "They won't let me in anymore. Mr. Vorhees took away my key."

Runyon made a sympathetic noise.

"I really liked working for him, you know? You ever see his yacht?"

"No."

"It's down a ways, this side." Beckett set off again in quick, jerky strides. After a couple of hundred yards he stopped and pointed. "There she is. Isn't she a beauty?"

Runyon looked. All he saw was a yacht—big, sleek, expensive. But in Beckett's eyes it was a pot of gold at the end of somebody else's rainbow. He said with a kind of wistful hunger, "Man, I wish I had a boat like that. Maritimo 73, eighty-one footer with a twenty-one foot beam, two Caterpillar C32 engines, thirty knots cruising speed. Sweet. But he doesn't take her out as often as he should. If I owned her, I'd be cruising all the time. All the time."

Runyon let him gawk a few more seconds before yanking him back to reality. "What did you want to talk to me about, Ken?"

"What? Oh, God." Beckett's thin features seemed to curl and reshape themselves, like a play-dough face being manipulated between unseen hands. Misery replaced the wistfulness in his eyes and voice.

"Something about your sister. Something you can't let her do."

"She has a gun now," Beckett said.

"A gun. What kind of gun?"

"Pistol. She never had one before, she never liked guns."

"Where did she get it?"

"I don't know. She wouldn't tell me when I found it. She said it was for protection, but she was lying. I can tell when she's lying. 'Don't you dare tell anybody, Kenny.' But a gun…I *couldn't* keep quiet, not after I heard her talking on the phone."

"Who was she talking to?"

"That bastard Chaleen. She's planning something bad with him, I know she is."

"Only you don't know exactly what."

"No. I was in the other room and her voice was low—I couldn't hear everything she said. Plans, she always has plans, but she won't tell me what they are. Chaleen, but not me. 'Everything will be all right, Kenny, you'll see. Haven't I always taken care of you?' No, she hasn't, not always. Not the way she should."

"Like letting you go to jail for a crime you didn't commit."

"Yes."

"What else?"

No response.

"Ask you to help her meet rich yachtsmen? Her ex-husbands, Andrew Vorhees."

"Oh, God. You know about her and Mr. Vorhees?"

Runyon nodded.

"I don't mind so much that she's fucking him," Beckett said. "He's okay, he always treated me decent, and we need the money. I understand that. But why does she have to have bastards like Chaleen, too? It's like a game with her...one and then another and then somebody else..."

"Does Mr. Vorhees know about her and Chaleen?"

"He'd be pissed if he did. Real pissed."

Runyon said, "Tell me exactly what you overheard Cory saying on the phone. Everything you can remember."

That mimicking falsetto again: "'Bitch deserves it for what she did. Careful, no mistakes. So much at stake for both of us, Frank.'"

"Who did she mean by 'bitch?'"

"Mrs. Vorhees."

"Mentioned her by name?"

"No, but I knew that's who it was."

Not conclusively, he didn't. "What else did she say? Anything about when whatever it is is going to happen? Or how?"

"Soon. Cory said that, soon. How? No."
Beckett drew a long, shaky breath. Then, in
a half whisper, "I don't want them to hurt
Mrs. Vorhees."

"Neither do I."

"That's why I called you, I didn't know
what else to do. Cory's done a lot of bad
things, but I never thought she was capable of…of…" The word *murder* was in his
mouth, his lips shaping it, but he couldn't
bring himself to say it aloud.

"Does she know you overheard her talking to Chaleen?"

"No. I almost told her, but…it wouldn't
have done any good. She'd've just lied. She
says she never lies to me but she does, all
the time. She lies to everybody." Another
shaky breath. "She's my sister, I love her,
but sometimes I think she's a little crazy…"

Runyon had nothing to say to that.

Beckett seemed to make an effort to
pull himself together. He said, "Mr. Runyon? Can you stop them from hurting Mrs.
Vorhees?"

"If we can." He got out a business card, one of those with both his cell and home numbers on it, and pressed it into Beckett's hand. "If you find out anything more, call me right away, day or night."

"Right away. Yes."

"And be careful not to let on to Cory that you've been talking to me."

"I won't. I mean I will."

Runyon left him standing there staring at the boats in the West Harbor slips, his mouth shaping more words that he couldn't or wouldn't speak aloud.

13.

I was home when Runyon reported in—
one of my out-of-the-office days devoted
to running errands, puttering, and spending time with my pulp magazine collection.
Kerry's recent promotion to vice president
of Bates and Carpenter kept her working
a full five-day week at the ad agency, plus
a fair amount of overtime, and with Emily
at school and then music practice—she had
her thirteen-year-old heart set on a singing
career—I usually had the condo to myself.
Which was all right with me. In this elec-
tronic age, most people can't seem to remain
unconnected for more than a few minutes,
as if they're afraid of being alone with their
thoughts. Not me. I've always felt comfort-
able by myself, alone with my thoughts.

I was trying to decide if I could afford a hundred bucks for a 1932 issue of
Dime Detective with an Erle Stanley Gard-

ner novelette, one of only two issues from that year that I didn't have. The price wasn't too bad on the current collector's market and the dealer making the offer was a man I'd bought from before; the sticking point was the magazine's condition, which he described as "near very good with a piece missing from the spine." He'd provided color scans in his e-mail, but looking at scans isn't the same thing as examining a magazine firsthand.

Jake's report put me in a quandary. I didn't blame him for talking to Kenneth Beckett—I'd have done the same if I'd been on the receiving end of the plea for help—but what he'd been told created an ethical and moral dilemma. Officially we had no standing in the matter. No client, no evidence to support the suspicions of an emotionally damaged young man, which for all we knew for certain were nothing more than delusional ravings. Nor could we justify notifying the police. If the allegations turned out to be unfounded, we'd be wide open for a ruinous lawsuit.

That was the ethical and legal side of it. The moral duty side was something else again. In all good conscience, you couldn't afford not to alert a potential victim when you had enough familiarity with the other people concerned to make premeditated homicide a very real possibility.

I hemmed and hawed with myself for a time. Then I called Tamara to get her take, mainly for support because I knew what her position would be. As young as she is, and despite a somewhat checkered past, she has a moral outlook similar to mine and Runyon's.

"Damn right we should do something," she said. "Sooner the better. I say take what we know to Margaret Vorhees and see what she says."

"What I was thinking, too."

"Maybe she'll hire us to protect her." Moral, my partner, but ever practical. "Yeah, I know we're not set up for bodyguard work, but we could make an exception in this case."

"If it comes to that, we'll consider it."

"Think I should be the one to talk to her, woman to woman?"

Tamara had plenty of strong points, but caution and tact were two that she hadn't quite mastered yet. And when you were dealing with a prominent citizen who was also a vindictive alcoholic, you had to be extra careful. I said, "Better let me do it. I'll need her phone numbers, land and cell both."

"No problem."

She had them for me in less than two minutes. I tried the cell number first, but the call went straight to voice mail. I clicked off without leaving a message and rang her home phone.

That call was answered by a woman with a Spanish accent who said she was the housekeeper. Mrs. Vorhees had left at nine o'clock to keep an appointment, she said, and wasn't expected back until mid-afternoon. I tapped out the cell number again and this time left a callback message, laying out my bona fides and using Cory and Kenneth Beckett's names to stress the necessity for a meeting.

Time passed. No callback.

The lack of response made me edgy. No good reason—socialites like Margaret Vorhees usually maintained a busy schedule and might not regularly check voice mail—but still the protracted silence didn't set well. At three o'clock I tried the Vorhees home again. Answering machine this time. I left another message. And then waited some more.

Four o'clock. Nothing.

Four-thirty. Emily came home with a friend and the two of them went into her room to work together on a homework assignment. Then Kerry called from Bates and Carpenter to say that an account meeting would keep her there until at least six-thirty. Would I do something about dinner? Sure I would. Pizza. Pepperoni and anchovy. We hadn't had one in a while.

Five-thirty. I'd been cooped up in the condo long enough, I decided. Might as well drive down to 24th Street and pick up the pizza at the restaurant, rather than calling ahead and having it delivered.

But once I was in the car, I let impulse turn me in the other direction, down Portero and then into St. Francis Wood. There was still plenty of time to collect the pizza before Kerry got home, and maybe Margaret Vorhees was at her house by now; might even have been there a while and for reasons of her own wasn't returning messages. Couldn't hurt to drive by and see.

14.

Like Nob Hill, St. Francis Wood, on the lower western slope of Mount Davidson, is one of the city's best neighborhoods: large old homes on large lots that you couldn't afford to buy unless your net worth was counted in the millions. The Vorhees house stood on a tree-shaded street not far from the home once owned by George Moscone, the San Francisco mayor who'd been assassinated along with Harvey Milk back in the '70s. Spanish Mission-style place, all stucco and dark wood and terra-cotta tile, tucked back behind tall hedges and a profusion of yucca trees. A line of eucalyptus ran along the west side, the trees' elongated shadows thickening inkily as night closed down. The overall effect was of a kind of mini-estate that had the effect of diminishing the stature of its neighbors.

Even with all the vegetation, I could see that the porch light was on and another burned behind one of the big front windows. Security lights, possibly, but they were enough to make me pull over and park next to the driveway.

The Wood is only a few miles from the ocean and a light fog was drifting in, just thick enough to wrap the tops of trees in faintly luminous skeins. The mist made the evening chilly; I pulled my coat collar up as I went through a gate in the front hedge.

Nobody answered the bell. I rang it four times, turned away, turned back, and set off the rolling chimes once more. Wasted effort. If Margaret Vorhees was home, she was neither receiving nor acknowledging visitors.

I turned back down off the porch, and as I did so, a hazy glow caught my eye across the side garden—a lighted window in the nearside wall of the garage. Well, maybe she was out there doing something. Might as well have a look.

A path led to the garage through a geo-
metrical arrangement of ornamental grasses
and shrubbery. I picked my way along until
I was about halfway, near enough to see that
the light behind the garage window had
an oddly unsteady, nebulous quality. That
was the first warning sign. The others came
quickly as I moved closer: a low, steady
rumbling inside the garage, just audible in
the night's stillness, then a faint acrid smell
that twitched my nostrils—familiar, too familiar. I broke into a run, the skin pulling
along the back of my neck.

There was a door next to the window,
midway along the wall, but it was locked
or jammed. When I put my face up close
to the glass, I was looking at swirling layers
of gray as if thick clouds of fog had been
trapped inside. Through them I could just
make out the shape of a low-slung sports
car, its engine throbbing like an erratic
pulse.

I ran around to the front, but there were
no outside handles on the double garage
doors: electronically controlled and locked

tight. Back fast to the side wall, where I broke the window with my elbow. The construction of the garage must have provided a tight seal; stinking waves of carbon monoxide came pouring out, driving me back and to one side.

With my head ducked low I threw my weight against the door, but all that got me was a wrenching shoulder pain. Then I did what I should have done in the first place: stepped back, drove the flat of my shoe into the panel next to the knob. The second time I did that, the lock tore loose and door scraped inward on the cement floor.

I shoved it all the way open, releasing more of the swirling poison, and plunged in blindly, holding my breath.

Despite the dull furry glow from an overhead light, I could barely see; the waves of exhaust burned my eyes, started them watering. I smacked into the car on the passenger side, bent to squint through the window. A figure was slumped over the wheel inside, but I couldn't make out whether it was a man or a woman. I fumbled around until I located the door handle. Locked. Clawed my way around to the driver's side. That door was locked, too.

The fumes had gotten into my lungs, tore the air out of them and started a burst of staccato coughing. No way I could stay in here now without putting myself at risk. I groped back around the car, stumbled out through the side door. Leaned against the garage wall, gulping until my head and chest cleared.

When I could breathe again without hacking, I dragged out my pencil flash and ran along the path to the house to hunt for a hose bib. Found one, soaked my handkerchief in cold water. The fumes were no longer quite as thick when I got back to the garage; I could see the car more clearly now, a black Mercedes job. I sucked in another breath, held the wet handkerchief over my mouth and nose, and pushed back inside.

First thing was to get the double doors open to let more of the monoxide empty out. I no longer felt any sense of urgency; as dense as the trapped fumes had been, the Mercedes' engine had been running a long time—much too long for the person slumped behind the wheel to still be alive. I splashed the walls with penlight until I located the switch that operated the automatic door opener. When the mechanism began to grind I turned back toward a workbench that stretched along one wall.

Tools hung neatly on a pegboard. Hammer...no, it'd take too long to break through safety glass on a Mercedes. Pry bar was what I needed...there, hanging behind a handsaw. Got it.

Coughing again, I managed to wedge the thin end of the bar into the crack next to the lock on the driver's door. Couldn't spring it at first, thought I'd have to use the bar to try breaking the glass, then gave it one more yank—and the door popped open.

I threw the bar down, leaned in past the slumped figure—a woman—and twisted the ignition key to cut off the wheezing rhythm of the engine. The woman and the car interior both stank of whiskey. I got both hands under her arms, dragged her limp body out of the car. My legs had a rubbery feel by the time I'd hauled her partway down the driveway; the drop to my knees beside her was as much a collapse as a willful lowering. My chest still burned, I felt sick to my stomach. Too damn old for this kind of thing.

Somebody started shouting out on the street, but I was too focused on the woman to pay much attention. Fortyish, red-gold hair cut short, eyes wide open with the whites showing, lips stretched wide and curled inward, the skin of her face a bright cherry red. No need to feel for a pulse, but I did it anyway. Too late, too goddamn late. Would've been too late even if I'd gotten here twenty or thirty minutes sooner.

I had never seen Margaret Vorhees before, but I had no doubt she was the dead woman even before I had it confirmed.

Running footsteps, two shouting voices now, a man and a woman. Neighbors, it turned out. The man made a 911 call on his cell phone, and a good thing he was there to do it. I didn't have enough breath left to speak above a cough-riddled whisper.

15.

I was all right again by the time the police and an EMT unit showed up, but the EMTs insisted on checking me over and giving me oxygen. Then there was the usual Q and A with a pair of patrolmen, and another of the same with an African-American inspector I knew slightly named Sam Davis. Why was I there? A business matter to discuss with Mrs. Vorhees. What sort of business matter? Information I'd come by pertaining to the theft of a valuable necklace of hers. Was I working for her? No, I'd never met the woman. The information had come into my possession through another case my agency was investigating. Could the case have any connection with her death? I didn't know, couldn't say.

After that I faded into the background while Davis and the forensics and coroner's people went about their work. On the front seat of the Mercedes they found Margaret Vorhees' purse, the remote unit that operated the garage doors, and a nearly empty bottle of Irish whiskey. According to the neighbors, she'd been drinking heavily since the separation from her husband. That opened up the possibility that she'd been despondent enough to take her own life, but what the police didn't find, either in the car or in the house, was anything resembling a suicide note. Which left the natural assumption that her death had been accidental. Alcoholic drives home from somewhere drunk, taking little nips of Irish on the way; pulls the car into the garage, presses the remote to lower the doors, then passes out with the engine still running. Stupid, tragic accident. Happens all the time.

But not this time.

My gut instinct said it was murder.

What Kenneth Beckett had overheard was part of the reason. But there was more than that. The monoxide business had a staged feel. The near empty whiskey bottle

on the front seat was just a little too conve-
nient; well-bred socialites, no matter how
alcoholic, are much less inclined to suck on
an open bottle while driving than your average drunk. Then there was the overhead
light in the garage; if she'd been out flitting
around somewhere in her Mercedes, why
would she have left it burning? Same with
the porch light and the lamp in the living
room. And the security system had been
switched off. No woman living alone is
likely to forget to arm hers when she leaves
the house.

None of the neighbors the cops talked
to had noticed anyone in the vicinity during the afternoon. Even if they had seen a
man who'd probably been an occasional if
not frequent visitor, it wouldn't seem sus-
picious. And it would've been easy enough
for that man to get Margaret Vorhees drunk
enough to pass out, carry her through the
jungly side yard to the garage, put her into
the Mercedes along with the props, start the
engine, set the snap lock on the side garage
door, and then walk away unseen.

A man named Frank Chaleen.

Working from a scheme designed by Cory Beckett.

But all of that was pure conjecture—the primary reason why I hedged with Sam Davis, didn't voice my suspicions. Without any clear evidence of foul play, I had nothing to offer except the ragged hearsay testimony of an unstable young man about to be tried for grand theft. Another thing: you learn to tread cautiously with the law in my business, if you want to stay in business. Cops like cooperation, but what they don't like are insupportable complications. In a case like this, the smart thing is to keep your mouth shut and let them come to their own conclusions.

But keeping silent was galling just the same. Even with a high profile victim like Margaret Vorhees, the police investigation was likely to be superficial. Andrew Vorhees had a lot of clout and unless he suspected foul play, which wasn't too likely, he'd want the case closed quickly and with the least amount of publicity. There didn't seem to be much doubt that the final verdict would be accidental death.

Which meant Cory Beckett and Frank Chaleen would get away with murder.

And there didn't seem to be any way to prevent it.

16.

Wrong one more time. We weren't through with the case after all.

Andrew Vorhees kept me in it the next morning. Tamara and Runyon were never really out. Once Tamara got her teeth into something like this, she was like a bulldog with a puzzling chew toy: kept picking at it, shaking it, trying to make sense of it. For Jake, it was the tenuous bond he'd forged with Kenneth Beckett and his concern for the kid's welfare.

The three of us held an early conference in Tamara's office. It seemed pretty clear now what Cory Beckett's plan was, we all agreed on that. Payback for the attempted frame-up was part of it, but the central motive was greed: with Margaret Vorhees out of the way, Cory had a clear shot at becoming the next Mrs. Vorhees. Marrying fat cats, as Tamara pointed out, had been her deal all along.

The timing of the murder was part of the plan, too: before her brother's trial. Once Margaret Vorhees was dead she could work on Vorhees to use his influence with the DA's office, get them to change their minds about prosecuting. That was why she'd been so confident Kenneth wouldn't go to prison.

Shifting the attempted frame to him had gotten her off the hook so she could plan her revenge, and also kept her from being a suspect if the police questioned the accident set-up. Only Kenneth had almost screwed it up for her by running away. Clearly she had no qualms about using him, but she still cared enough not to want him suspected, either—her main reason for hiring us to find him and bring him back. It was a safe bet she'd have alibis fixed up for the two of them last night, just in case.

Cory had used sex at first to hook Chaleen into the scheme, but we figured his primary motive was the same as hers: greed.

A big cash payoff once she was married to Vorhees. As Tamara said, "Chaleen's the kind of dude who'll do anything if there's enough money in it. Just like Cory. Risk takers. Do whatever's necessary for the big prize."

I asked Runyon how he thought Kenneth Beckett would react to the news of Margaret Vorhees' death.

"Hard to tell," he said. "He'll suspect his sister and Chaleen were responsible, but because it looks like an accident he can't be sure. If he accuses her she'll just stonewall him."

"Could he crack, go to the police?"

"Not likely."

"Come back to you for help?"

"Maybe. And maybe I shouldn't wait to find out."

"Cory won't let you talk to him, if that's what you're thinking."

"She might not have anything to say about it," Runyon said.

And that was when the call from Andrew Vorhees' office came in.

Tamara answered it, listened, raised an eyebrow in my direction, listened some more, said, "I'll see if he's available," and clapped her hand over the mouthpiece. "Andrew Vorhees' secretary," she said to me. "Man wants to see you ASAP."

Well, I might have expected it, though not this soon. I took the call and agreed to a meeting with Vorhees in his office at eleven.

Tamara said when I ended the conversation, "His wife dies last night, he's in his office bright and early this morning. Business as usual."

"He'd say it was his way of keeping his mind off his loss."

"Yeah, sure. What're you gonna tell him when he asks why you were out at his house?"

"Nothing about the monoxide job being murder. There's another way to handle it."

"What way?"

"By rocking the boat Cory Beckett doesn't want rocked," I said. "If I work it right, I might even be able to punch enough holes to sink it."

17.
Jake Runyon

Kenneth Beckett's fragile mental state was one thing that worried him. The other was the gun Cory Beckett had gotten her hands on.

Why had a woman who'd never owned a handgun all of a sudden decided she needed one? Not to use on Margaret Vorhees, as Kenneth had been afraid of, so there had to be another reason. Protection made sense only if she was being threatened by somebody. Chaleen, Vorhees? Possible. Or was the gun necessary for some new scheme she was cooking up?

Too many questions, too few answers. Frustrating as hell. Runyon didn't particularly like being thrust into the role of father confessor to an emotionally damaged twenty-four-year-old, but he felt sorry for Beckett, didn't want to see him hurt or used any more than he'd already been. But the only way to help him was to free him from his sister's domination, and that couldn't be done without Beckett's cooperation. And a better understanding of what the woman was up to, something else it seemed only Kenneth could supply.

When Runyon left the agency he drove down to the St. Francis Yacht Club. Maybe Beckett would contact him again, maybe he wouldn't; it depended on any number of things—his confused emotions, how much resistance he had to his sister's control, whether or not he'd told her that he'd been confiding in the detective who'd tracked him down. Runyon didn't like the idea of waiting to find out. Which left trying to initiate another face-to-face meeting himself.

Small chance Cory would let her brother out alone so soon after Margaret Vorhees' death, but if she had, he'd be somewhere near the yacht club. He wasn't. Runyon prowled the basin area long enough to be sure, then made a couple of slow futile passes back and forth along Marina Boulevard. That was all the hanging around he allowed himself; he had other agency business to attend to.

His cell phone vibrated once after he left the Marina, twice more during the course of his day. None of the calls was from Kenneth Beckett.

18.

When you faced Andrew Vorhees in his plush Civic Center office, it was easy enough to see how he'd been able to forge a successful political and business career despite his scandal-ridden private life. He cut an imposing figure behind a broad cherry-wood desk: lean, athletic body encased in a black silk suit that must have cost a couple of thousand dollars, thick dark-curled hair whitening at the temples, craggy features, piercing brown eyes. The kind of self-confident, strong-willed man who dominates most any room he's in.

He wore a tight, solemn expression this morning, but there was no other evidence that he might be grieving. If he'd had any feelings left for his dead wife, they were well concealed. When I said, "I'm sorry for your loss, Mr. Vorhees," while we were shaking hands, he made a vague gesture as if I'd expressed sorrow over the fact that the weather wasn't better today. He held on to my hand for a few seconds while his eyes looked into mine: trying to read me and at the same time let me know he was the alpha male here. I showed him about as much of the inner man as he was showing me, and that I was not intimidated by him.

The first thing he said after we were seated was, "I've never met a private detective before." He didn't quite make the words "private detective" sound like an indictment, but close enough.

"A business like any other," I said.

He picked up a turquoise-and-silver letter opener, held it between thumb and forefinger and tipped it in my direction. Bluntly he asked, "Were you working for my wife?"

"No. I never had any dealings with her. As a matter of fact, I never met her."

"Then what were you doing at my home last night?"

"I went there to talk to her about some things I felt concerned her."

"What things?"

"Relationships, mainly."

"Margaret and I were separated—I suppose you know that."

"I'd heard as much."

"Well?"

"Not your relationship with your wife. Yours with Cory Beckett."

Vorhees' spine stiffened a little. He made another jabbing motion with the letter opener before he said, "Even if that were true, my private life is none of your business. Nor was it any of my wife's business. I told you, we were legally separated."

"Are you denying a relationship with Cory Beckett?"

"I don't have to confirm or deny anything to you."

"No, you don't. But it so happens I saw you coming out of her apartment building the other day. I mentioned it to her, but evidently she didn't mention it to you."

She hadn't. His poker face wasn't quite good enough to hide the fact. "What were you doing there?"

"She was my client at the time. I don't have to tell you she hired my agency to find her brother when he disappeared two weeks ago. One reason I went to see her that day was to inform her we'd located him."

"One reason?"

"The other is that I don't like being lied to."

"Lied to about what?"

"Why don't you ask her?"

"I'm asking you."

"The theft her brother's charged with," I said. "The fact that it was a frame-up and she was the intended target, not him. The fact that it was her idea for him to take the blame and that she had help having it done."

Vorhees' reaction to that was a scowl that created rows of vertical lines like fissures across his forehead. He let the letter opener drop with a little clatter on the desktop.

"Bullshit," he said.

"Fact."

"How could you know all that?"

"I'm a detective, remember?"

"Why would Cory want to frame her brother?"

"Ask her."

"The hell I will," Vorhees said. "I don't believe it. She loves him, she's doing everything she can to get him off. She'd have to be crazy to do what you're accusing her of."

"Or sane and scheming."

"Scheming? To do what?"

"I can't give you an answer to that question. Aren't you going to ask me who arranged the frame in the first place?"

"If I thought it was true, I wouldn't have to ask."

"Or who helped Cory shift it to her brother?"

"…All right. Who?"

"The same person who was recruited to frame her."

"Goddamn it, who?"

"Frank Chaleen."

The name rocked him like a blow. He got abruptly to his feet, stood woodenly for

a clutch of seconds, then flattened his hands
on the desktop and leaned toward me.

"Bullshit," he said again.

"Fact," I repeated.

"She hardly knows Chaleen."

"She knows him a lot better than you
think."

"How do you know she does?"

"He was with her when she went up to
the Petaluma River to pick up her brother.
Our operative was there and talked to both
of them. Talked to Kenneth, too. He'll confirm it for you if you like."

Vorhees didn't say anything.

I took a chance and pushed the enve-
lope as far as I was willing to. "Chaleen gets
around, doesn't he? One woman at a time's
not enough for him. Wives and mistresses,
both fair game."

"What the hell does that mean?"

"What do you think it means, given his
involvement in the original plan to frame
Cory Beckett?"

Vorhees said between his teeth, "That son of a bitch! I'll make him wish he was never born."

I let that pass without comment.

The sudden fury had turned his face blood-dark, made a vein jump on one temple, but it didn't last long. He hadn't gotten where he was by letting his emotions run away with him. I watched him make a visible effort to control himself. At length he said, "You better not be lying to me about any of this."

"I'm not lying."

He lowered himself into his chair, folded his hands together. All business again. "I've got enough to deal with as it is without the media busting my chops again," he said. "What would it take for you to keep all of this quiet?"

"Are you offering me a bribe, Mr. Vorhees?"

"No. A favor for a favor. I have a fair amount of influence in this city. I could do you some good—"

"No, you couldn't. You can't trade for or buy my silence. You already know that if you've checked me out and I'm sure you have. But I'll give it to you for nothing. I didn't intend to make trouble for your wife and I don't intend to make trouble for you. That's not why I confided in you."

"No? Then why did you?"

"I don't like to see anybody jerked around by lovers and former friends. Particularly a newly bereaved husband."

"You expect me to believe that?"

"Believe what you like." I got to my feet. "I've said my piece—it's in your hands now."

He made a derisive noise. But his face was set now, hard and brittle, like a ceramic sculpture fresh out of the kiln. Accepting it finally, I thought, his denial chipping off from around the core of truth. Redirecting his simmering anger from me to where it belonged.

Mission accomplished.

Boat rocked and holed and taking on water, fast.

19.
Jake Runyon

Seven-fifteen that night, and Runyon had just come out of a Chinese restaurant on Taraval. Chinese food had been Colleen's favorite; they'd eaten it two or three times a week during their twenty years together. After she was gone he'd kept up the ritual as a way to hold on to the memory of the good times they'd shared. But since he'd met Bryn, he ate Chinese less often and only on those nights when he was alone. Progress of a sort, he supposed. Getting on with his life. But he'd never give up the ritual entirely; every time he lifted a forkful of moo shu pork or sesame chicken, he visualized Colleen's smile and felt her there close to him again.

He was keying open the door to his Ford when Kenneth Beckett contacted him again.

"Margaret Vorhees is dead, Mr. Runyon," the kid's voice said without preamble.

"Yes, I know."

"I don't think it was an accident. Chaleen did it. Cory was with me and Mr. Vorhees last night, but she…the two of them… I told you, didn't I? You said you wouldn't let it happen."

Runyon sidestepped that. "Does Cory know what you suspect?"

"No. She'd just lie if I told her. She never used to lie to me, now she does it all the time. She keeps saying after the trial tomorrow everything will be like it used to, but that's a lie, too. It's only going to get worse."

"Why do you say that?"

"Mrs. Vorhees…that wasn't the end of it."

"You think Cory's planning something else?"

Six-beat. Background noise filtered through the silence: music, the low mutter of voices. Then, "Yes. Something."

"You have any idea what?"

"No."

"Any way you can find out?"

"How? She won't tell me anything."

"Listen to me, Ken, this is important. Do you know where she keeps the gun you told me about?"

"Gun? Oh God, the gun…"

"Can you find it, get rid of it somehow?"

No response.

"Ken?" Runyon said. "Can you get rid of the gun?"

"…I don't know."

Too difficult trying to get through to him on the phone. "All right. Where are you calling from?"

"A bar down the block. Mr. Vorhees came to the apartment a while ago. He was mad, real mad—he knows about Cory fucking Chaleen. He kept yelling at her, calling her names. I couldn't stand to listen so I left and came here."

"What's the name of the bar?"

"…A bar, I don't know."

"Ask somebody. I'll come there and we'll talk some more. Decide what to do."

The bar sounds cut off—Beckett must have put his hand over the mouthpiece. Then, after close to a minute, "It's Shanahan's. On Pine Street."

"It shouldn't take me more than half an hour. Wait for me."

The Ford's GPS got him there and into a legal parking space in twenty-seven minutes. Shanahan's was an upscale Nob Hill tavern masquerading as an Irish pub, with maybe a dozen patrons at the bar and in booths.

None of them was Kenneth Beckett.

Wasted trip. Runyon checked the men's room to make sure, then spoke briefly to the barman and a couple of customers. Nobody remembered Beckett. Faded in, made his call, faded out. Like a shadow.

No, like a moth. Fluttering back and forth, going nowhere. And unable to resist the pull of a destructive flame.

20.

The result of Kenneth Beckett's trial date
appearance was what his sister planned it to
be. In view of the fact that the complainant
was recently deceased, the DA's office decided not to pursue prosecution. That was
the reason the ADA gave the judge for the
nolle prosequi, anyhow. It may have been
that Andrew Vorhees had used his influence after all, but if so, he hadn't followed it
up by attending the trial. It also may have
been that the DA figured he couldn't make
any political hay off the case and would
look better in the public eye if he backed
off. Whatever the reason, Beckett was off
the hook with nothing more than a judicial
warning.

The details came from Runyon, who
was there—the only other person present
aside from the Becketts, the legal eagles,
and a couple of reporters looking for and

not finding an angle they could use to stir up fresh interest in a socialite's "accidental" death. He'd figured he might have a chance to talk to Kenneth, but Cory saw to it that that didn't happen. She hustled her brother into the courtroom, and then out again, with Sam Wasserman helping her run interference. The two reporters didn't get near him, either.

Tamara was keeping an Internet watch on the principals, but there were no further developments that day or most of the next. Whatever Vorhees intended to do about Cory Beckett and Frank Chaleen, he either hadn't done it yet or was doing it so quietly no word leaked out. And there was no further word on what Cory might be scheming with or without her newly acquired pistol.

Then came late afternoon, the day after the trial.

I was in my office writing a case report on a routine insurance fraud investigation. I'd written scores like it before, but today for some reason I was having trouble getting it down in coherent English. Committing words to paper, or now to a computer screen, is not one of my long suits; I have to drag them together into intelligible sentences at the best of times, and this wasn't one of the best. I was staring off into space, trying to think of a way to frame what should have been a simple statement of fact, when the outer door to the anteroom opened.

Except that it didn't just open; it thumped and rattled as if it had been pushed hard. Sharp clicking steps followed. I couldn't see who'd come in because my office door was partly closed. Alex Chavez was at one of the anteroom desks writing a report of his own, and I heard the mutter of his voice and then a loud and angry response. Even before Alex came and poked his head in and said I had a visitor, I knew who it was.

She was standing alone in the middle of the anteroom, straight as a tree with her arms down at her sides and her mouth so tightly compressed it seemed lipless. Dressed all in expensive red today—suit, shoes, scarf, purse, the scarlet color scheme broken only by a white cashmere turtleneck and a gold cameo brooch. This was the other Cory Beckett, the real Cory Beckett. Nothing soft or seductive about her. Hard. Glacial. All the fire burned deep inside—a molten core wrapped in a block of ice.

Chavez sat looking at her from a distance with his mouth open a little, as if he'd never seen anyone quite like her before. Tamara was there, too, standing in the door of her office; she glanced at me as I stepped out, but only for a second. Cory Beckett had her full attention. She didn't have to have met the woman before to know who she was.

Cory's magnetic gaze was fixed on me, unblinking, as I approached her. Subzero cubes shining with a black hatred. Touch her skin, I thought, and you'd burn your fingers. Like touching dry ice.

I said, "Well, Miss Beckett. This is a surprise."

"Is it?" Her voice had a hoarse quality, as if it, too, were partially frozen. "I don't think so, after what you did."

"What do you think I did?"

"Don't play games with me. Your lies to Andrew Vorhees almost cost my brother his freedom."

"They weren't my lies. They're yours."

"I ought to sue you for slander."

"But you won't because you know you have no case. I never accused you of anything, or even once took your name in vain. Ask Vorhees, if you haven't already."

Her mouth worked and twisted as if she were about to spit in my face. I wouldn't have been surprised if she had. Instead she said, "Damn you, you still could've been responsible for Kenny going to prison."

"But it didn't happen. You seemed confident he'd get off, and you managed to maneuver it so he did?"

"No thanks to you."

"How's your relationship going with Andrew Vorhees, by the way? Wedding bells in the offing? After a decent period of mourning, of course."

No reaction. Cory Ice. She stood there shredding me with those eyes, a staredown that went on for maybe fifteen seconds. Then she did the one thing I wasn't expecting—the thing, I realized afterward, she'd come here to do.

Without warning, cat-quick, she belted me open-handed across the face.

It was a hell of a blow. She was no lightweight; there was considerable strength in that slender body. I staggered backward a step, bells going off in my head, before I regained my equilibrium. She stayed put long enough to watch with chilly satisfaction as I lifted a hand, grimacing, and then she spun on her heel and stalked out.

Chavez, still gawking, murmured something in Spanish. Even Tamara was impressed. She said from her office doorway, "Wow, that was some slap. You okay?"

My cheek stung like fury. Just touching it made me wince. "I'll live."

"You're lucky the bitch didn't use her nails."

"Yeah," I said. "Or her gun."

21.
Jake Runyon

It all came to a head three days later.

Suddenly and violently.

He was working Sunday afternoon, late, doing one of the few kinds of jobs he disliked because it involved spy photography: staked out near a Belmont house owned by a man named Garza who had a large accident policy with Northwestern Insurance. Garza had put in a claim, citing an on-the-job back injury that kept him from doing any sort of manual labor, and had a doctor's report to back him up. But Northwestern smelled fraud and hired the agency to investigate, with Runyon getting the assignment. Fraud was what it was. He'd found out that Garza and the doctor were old high school buddies who played golf together now and then, and now here he was with his Nikon digital camera, looking to record proof that the subject wasn't as incapacitated as he claimed.

Getting it, too. Garza was too smart to do any heavy work at his plumbing supply business, but he must have figured he was safe enough, it being Sunday, to do some at home. He was having a new driveway put in, and evidently he'd decided to cut costs by doing part of the job himself. So there he was, shoveling and spreading gravel without strain or pain, when Runyon drove by. Runyon had three clear shots, and was just framing another for good measure, when Kenneth Beckett called for the third and last time.

"Help me, Mr. Runyon. Please. I don't want to do it."

The voice, barely above a whisper, put him on instant alert. "I don't understand. What don't you want to do?"

"She said I have to, but I...I can't, it's not right."

"Talk to me, Ken. What isn't right?"

"Hurting somebody. Even a bastard like him."

"Who? Chaleen?"

"Yes."

"Then don't do it. You hear me?"

Breathy silence.

"Where are you?"

"His place."

"Where he lives?"

"He's in there. Alone. She...she said
I..."

"Home, office, *where*?"

"Office."

"All right. Stay where you are, don't go
near him, don't do anything. I'll be there as
soon as I can. You understand?"

He was talking to himself. The line
hummed emptily.

The only office Chaleen had, according
to the information Tamara had pulled up,
was at the packing materials company he
owned. Chaleen Manufacturing was somewhere on the southeastern side of the city,
near the Islais Creek Channel, but Runyon
couldn't remember the street name or address. He programmed the company name
into the GPS. Basin Street. Number 44.

It took him twenty minutes of fast driving to get there. Industrial area, dead quiet and deserted on a Sunday afternoon near dusk. Basin Street ran at an angle off Evans: four blocks long and lined with small manufacturing and warehousing companies, an auto-body shop, an outfit that made statuary for gardens and cemeteries, and midway along the last block, Chaleen Manufacturing.

There was no sign of the blue Dodge van; the street was empty of vehicles of any kind.

The kid hadn't waited this time, either. Back to the flame again.

Chaleen Manufacturing was a pair of buildings crowded behind a chain-link fence topped by strands of barbed wire. Sodium vapor nightlights, already burning, laid a faint greenish tinge over the grounds. The primary structure was an L-shaped hunk of corrugated iron; the much smaller building, a squat trailer-like affair that sat behind and to one side like a broken-off piece of the factory, had to be the office.

There were two double gates in the fence—truck-wide ones that opened into the yard and fronted a trio of loading bays, another set farther along that serviced the office. Light showed in one window of the squat building. And drawn up in the shadows next to it was a newish black Cadillac.

Runyon pulled up in front of the office gates. Before he got out he unlocked the glove compartment, transferred his .357 Magnum from its chamois wrapping to his coat pocket. In an area like this at nightfall, facing an unknown situation, he felt better having it handy.

A chill bay wind played with scraps of litter, swirling them along the uneven pavement, forming little heaps against the bottom of the fence; a fast-food bag slapped his leg as he stepped up to the closed gates. Closed, but not locked: the big Yale used to padlock them hung open from one of the links. He pushed through, his steps echoing hollowly on the arc-lit pavement.

The entrance door to the office building was also unlocked. He looked into a lighted outer office that appeared to be empty. Without entering he called Chaleen's name.

No answer.

Once more, shouting the name this time. Still no answer.

He went in then, leaving the door standing open behind him, one hand on the Magnum in his coat pocket. Two inner doors were closed. The first one he tried led to a dark storage room. He opened the second a crack, saw that the room beyond was also lighted, and called out again. Nothing but the faint afterecho of his own voice. He widened the crack so he could see what lay beyond.

Private office, large enough to take up most of the back half of the building. Desk, chairs, wet bar, couch, a shaded lamp on the desk providing the light.

And Frank Chaleen sitting in a backward sprawl on the couch, head flung back, eyes shut, one arm dangling over the side.

At first Runyon thought he was dead. But there was no blood or other signs of violence on Chaleen or the cushions under him, and as he moved closer he could hear the faint rasp of the man's breathing. He lifted one limp hand, pressed his thumb against the wrist artery. Pulse strong enough, if a little thready.

Passed out drunk was the way it looked; you could detect the odor of liquor on his breath, and on a table next to the couch was a nearly empty glass of what smelled like bourbon. But that wasn't the way it was. Chaleen had been drinking, all right, but he hadn't been doing it alone. The faintest lingering whiff of perfume verified that.

Cory's neat little set-up. Arranged a meeting on some pretext or other, slipped a heavy dose of something like Xanax or Valium into his glass of whiskey, stayed until it hit him, and then left him here unconscious to await execution.

I don't want to do it. She said I have to, but I...I can't...

No, Beckett couldn't. She'd underestimated her power to manipulate him into an act of violence he was constitutionally incapable of. But he'd been in here, and maybe he'd come close: the pillow resting on Chaleen's lap as if it had been dropped there; the partly crumpled piece of paper on the floor next to the couch, likely flung down before he ran out.

Runyon picked up the paper, smoothed it out. 8-1/2 x 11 company letterhead with two lines of computer typing on it and Chaleen's scrawled signature at the bottom. But he hadn't typed it and he hadn't signed it.

I can't keep on living. I've done too many things I'm ashamed of, hurt too many people. This is best for everybody.

The hell it was. Best for Cory. Only Cory.

Runyon shoved the phony suicide note into his pocket, turned for the door. There was nothing more for him to do here. Chaleen was no longer in any danger; he'd wake up before too much more time passed.

Runyon was in the car and on his way out of Basin Street before he called Bill's home number. Kerry answered, but Bill was there; Runyon gave him a terse report when he came on the line. Bill said, "Where do you think Beckett went, Jake? Back to the apartment?"

"He's got nowhere else to go."

"No telling what she might do when she hears Chaleen's still alive."

"I know it. I'm on my way there right now."

"Intervention?"

"I've got to try for his sake. I'll take full responsibility—"

"No, you won't. I'll meet you there, we'll handle it together."

22.

I had a shorter distance to travel, so I arrived at the Nob Hill address ahead of Runyon. Beckett's van wasn't anywhere on the street, but that didn't mean anything. The neighborhood has a smattering of small parking garages where residents pay outlandish monthly fees to park their vehicles. I'd left my car in the nearest one, the hell with the expense.

While I waited I paced the sidewalk in front, looking up at the lighted windows of the Beckett apartment. No telling for sure if both of them were up there; the curtains were closed. I wondered if Runyon and I were going to have trouble getting in, first to the building and then to the apartment. We couldn't go barreling through doors like a couple of commandos; admission had to be by permission.

I was not looking forward to the face-off…if we even got that far. We had plenty of ammunition, but none of it was much good from a legal standpoint unless Kenneth Beckett cracked and broke. Our position was still shaky; we had to be extra careful—no direct accusations, nothing in the least actionable without support from him. If he sided with his sister, we'd have another difficult decision to make: cops or no cops. Frank Chaleen wouldn't be any help; even if he believed he'd been drugged and set up, he wouldn't incriminate himself in a homicide.

I'd been there about ten minutes when Runyon came loping up the block. We conferred in the foyer while he leaned on the bell. I expected it to be a while before we got a response, and that the first thing we'd hear was a voice on the intercom. But it was only a few seconds before the door buzzer went off, while the intercom stayed silent.

Neither Runyon nor I said anything on the way inside. I could feel a sharpening tension. Nothing either of the Becketts did was completely predictable, it seemed.

The door to their apartment stood ajar. That ratcheted up the tension another notch. The sudden tight feeling in my gut was one I'd had before, a sixth sense warning sign that said: *Something wrong here.* From the look on Runyon's face, he felt it, too.

We went in slow and cautious, Jake announcing us. Kenneth Beckett answered in a flat, toneless voice: "Here, Mr. Runyon."

He was alone in the gaudily decorated living room, sitting rigidly on a chair in front of one of the gold-flecked mirrors, hands flat on his knees, eyes unblinking as they moved past Runyon to me. If he saw me at all, he didn't care who I was or why I was there. Those eyes—dark, lightless, like burned-out bulbs—confirmed my gut feeling of wrongness. So did two long, fresh scratches below his left cheekbone, the blood from them still oozing a little.

Runyon said to him, "Why didn't you wait for me at Chaleen's?"

"Cory." Then again, more a lament than an answer: "Cory. Cory."

"Where is she?"

"I'm sorry. Oh God, I'm sorry."

"Where, Ken?"

Beckett lifted one hand in a vague, loose gesture, then let it fall back onto his lap. Closed his eyes and sat there mute.

I moved first, taking the lead. The kitchen and dining rooms were empty. So was the first bedroom, hers, that opened off a central hallway. The adjacent bathroom was where we found her. Luxury bathroom with a sunken tub and a glass-block shower stall, the air moist as if a bath or shower had been taken not long ago and thick with the odors of soap and body oils.

And cordite. And blood.

I smelled the cordite as soon as I entered the bedroom, in time to gird myself before Runyon and I crossed over far enough to see the body. She lay sprawled on her back on a fuzzy black rug in front of the shower stall, a bright yellow robe covering her from neck to ankles. Alive, she'd been beautiful;

dead, she was a torn and ugly travesty. The bullet had gone in under her chin at an upward angle, ripped through the side of her face and opened up her head above the temple. The stall door and the glass blocks were streaked and spattered with blood, bone splinters, brain matter, the blood still wet and glistening. Dead less than half an hour.

Runyon said between his teeth, "Goddamn it, *why* didn't he stay at Chaleen's?"

There was nothing to say to that. My stomach was kicking like crazy; I'd seen dead bodies before, the aftermath of violence in too damn many forms, but I had never become inured to the sight. The reaction was always the same: sickness and disgust mingled with sadness and an impotent anger at the inhumanity of it.

The gun was on the floor next to the body, a short-barreled .38 with pearl grips. Neither Runyon nor I touched it. We backed out of there, returned to the living room.

Kenneth Beckett was still sitting in the same rigid posture, but his face was no longer impassive. Muscles moved beneath the skin, making his features shift and change shape like an image in a kaleidoscope. Tears leaked from the lifeless eyes, mixing with the blood from the scratches to form a reddish trail on one cheek. Soundless weeping.

Runyon went over to him, said his name twice to get his attention. "Have you called the police?"

"No. I couldn't. I thought you'd come, so I just…waited."

My cue to make the 911 call. But even as I spoke to the police dispatcher, I could hear what the two of them were saying to each other, Beckett in that same empty voice.

"What happened, Ken?"

"I killed her."

"Not deliberately. You wouldn't do that."

"No. Never. Never."

"Tell us what happened."

"Mad at me because I couldn't shoot Chaleen. Screamed at me, called me names. 'Give me the gun,' she said, 'I'll do it myself.' I didn't want to. She hit me, scratched me. That fucking gun. She yanked it out of my pocket. I tried to take it back and it… went off and she…she…" His eyes squeezed shut, then popped open wide like eyes in a Keane painting. "I killed her. I loved her and I killed her. I wish I was dead, too. But I couldn't make myself do that, either."

Death wish already granted, I thought. In a very real sense he'd died, too, the instant the bullet tore the life out of his sister.

Runyon said, "Why did she want Chaleen killed?"

"Kill or be killed, she said. Then we'd be safe. Safe."

Maybe Chaleen had threatened her, or maybe she'd decided if she got rid of him it would help salvage her relationship with Vorhees and her marriage plans. She had to've promised Chaleen plenty to do her dirty work for her and she wasn't the kind to share the wealth if it could be avoided.

"I tried to tell her I couldn't do it," Beckett was saying. "But she wouldn't take no for an answer. She never took no for an answer. I loved her so much, I always did what she wanted me to. In the light or in the dark. Only I couldn't this time, I just couldn't."

"What do you mean, in the dark?"

"In bed. At night."

"…You and Cory?"

"It wasn't wrong. She said so the first night she came into my room. It wasn't wrong because we loved each other."

"How old were you that first night?"

"Fifteen."

Runyon and I traded looks. Neither of us had seen this coming, yet we should have. The kind of woman Cory Beckett had been, the screwed-up mess Kenneth was. Sex had been her primary weapon, and she'd wielded it mercilessly with the men in her life. But sweet Jesus, her own brother.

"Only I wasn't enough for her. She had to have all those others. I didn't mind so much until Hutchinson. It wasn't the same with her after him. Because she wasn't the same."

Hutchinson. The biker felon she'd taken up with in Riverside, the one who'd been shot and killed by police.

"He talked her into it," Beckett said. "She said it was her idea, but it wasn't. He made her do it."

"Do what?"

"I couldn't stand looking at her afterward. But I couldn't stop fucking her, she wouldn't let me stop."

"Ken. What did Hutchinson make her do?"

"But only in the dark. I couldn't stand seeing her the way she was in the light. That's why I covered her in the bathroom after I killed her. I...couldn't...stand..."

Runyon asked the question again, but Beckett was no longer listening. His facial muscles stopped ticking and twitching, his tear-stained features smoothing out so that he looked about the age he'd been when his sister seduced him—a battered, crippled, very old fifteen. He sat staring sightlessly, his mouth moving but no words coming out. Lost now somewhere deep inside himself.

But Runyon and I couldn't just stand there and wait for the police. I wish we had. It would have been better for both of us if we hadn't let Beckett's last words send us back into that bloody bathroom.

We stood looking down at what was left of Cory Beckett. One fold of the yellow robe, I noticed then, had been draped over the other, the belt untied. I could not quite bring myself to reach down and open the robe. It was Runyon, after a few seconds, who did that.

It takes a lot to shock men who have been around as long as we have, but what we saw revealed, the reason why she'd always worn clothing that covered her to the neck, rocked us both. Runyon was not given to emotional outbursts; his whispered "Christ!" was a measure of how affected he was. All I could do was stand there in gaping silence.

Cory Beckett, femme fatale. The incestuous relationship with her brother was one of the new and terrible angles she'd brought to the role. This was the other, and in a way it was even worse.

She was tattooed.

One single massive tattoo, the entire front of her torso used as a canvas to portray a scene out of Dante's Inferno.

In intricate detail the upthrust breasts had been turned into a pair of erupting volcanoes, the nipples so violently colored they resembled volcanic cores. And spilling down over both globes, down over her belly to meet at her shaved pubis and disappear into the hollow between her legs, was a trail of molten fire.

It was the kind of voluntary sexual mutilation that could drive some men wild with lust, make them easier to manipulate and control.

And easier to destroy.